"We could get married."

"What?"

"Consider it a business deal. I have a trust fund that I can only tap into after being married for a year."

Ruth's head throbbed. She knew nothing about this man, other than he had a trust fund and he was a distant relative of Nora's.

"Look, you don't have to answer now. Just think about it. A working relationship is all I'm suggesting. The marriage certificate would simply satisfy the terms of the trust. We can specify the marriage be annulled once the loan is paid in a year's time."

"Will that matter? A marriage deal instead of a real one?" Ruth couldn't believe she was entertaining the idea.

Bo chuckled. "The terms of the trust weren't specific as to what kind of marriage, only that it's a legal one. It won't matter."

Marriage mattered to her. Marriage was sacred. It wasn't to be entered into lightly.

Clearing her throat, she managed a rough-sounding response. "I need some time to consider your offer."

Jenna Mindel lives in Northwest Lower Michigan with her husband and their dogs, where she enjoys the Great Lakes, the outdoors and strong coffee. Her love of fairy tales as a kid paved the way for Jenna to eventually create her own happily-ever-after stories. Her passion grew into writing flawed characters who realize their need to trust God before they can trust each other. Contact Jenna through her website, www.jennamindel.com.

Visit the Author Profile page at LoveInspired.com.

A Secret Christmas Family

Jenna Mindel

LOVE INSPIRED

INSPIRATIONAL ROMANCE

LOVE INSPIRED®

INSPIRATIONAL ROMANCE

PLEASE RECYCLE
THIS PRODUCT IS RECYCLABLE

Recycling programs
for this product may
not exist in your area.

ISBN-13: 978-1-335-58619-3

A Secret Christmas Family

Copyright © 2022 by Jenna Mindel

This is a work of fiction. Names, characters, places and incidents are either the product of the author's imagination or are used fictitiously. Any resemblance to actual persons, living or dead, businesses, companies, events or locales is entirely coincidental.

For questions and comments about the quality of this book, please contact us at CustomerService@Harlequin.com.

Love Inspired
22 Adelaide St. West, 41st Floor
Toronto, Ontario M5H 4E3, Canada
www.LoveInspired.com

Printed in U.S.A.

Ruth the Moabitess, the wife of Mahlon,
have I purchased to be my wife, to raise up
the name of the dead upon his inheritance, that
the name of the dead be not cut off from among
his brethren, and from the gate of his place.
—*Ruth* 4:10

For Abby, Lydia and Anna.
My romance movie peeps!

Chapter One

Burnt orange and golden-colored leaves swirled in the driveway from a balmy breeze. It might be warm for the first day of October, but Ruth Miller knew colder days were right around the corner. Autumn colors came early in the Upper Peninsula of Michigan; but then, winter did too. Especially on the eastern edge of Marquette County, where she lived in the middle-of-nowhere small town of Pine.

Her first winter alone. Her first Christmas without her husband of eleven years.

She shivered despite the seventy-degree day. She'd ordered wood in preparation for winter, but it lay in a pile, waiting to be stacked under the lean-to off the garage. She and Cole used to arrange the logs together, stacking them tight. Not this time. Not ever again. Pain shot through her as the reality of her loss burned anew.

It's not that she ever forgot Cole's death. Not

a day went by that she didn't think of him, but certain memories snuck up on her and stole her breath away. Like now, seeing that pile of firewood. Widowed nine weeks and three days, Ruth faced a year ahead that would be littered with firsts and never agains.

Swallowing hard, Ruth walked to the side door of her house and ran her fingers over the clapboard siding. It was due for a fresh swipe of white paint. This past spring, she and Cole had installed a wooden picket fence around their tiny backyard. It needed paint too. One more task to add to her swelling list of things to do.

Ruth entered the large mudroom that housed her washer and dryer. Her two boys' newly purchased tennis shoes still lay where they'd kicked them off last night when she'd called them inside for dinner. She should have made them change into their old ones after school, but she couldn't find the gumption. This morning, she hadn't bothered to correct them when they wore their old sneaks to school. Big picture, sneakers didn't matter much.

Glancing at the crisp white wainscoting on the lower half of the walls that matched the white cupboards her husband had installed over the laundry area, she gave in to despair. This was the house she and Cole had bought soon after they'd married. There were so many memories here—renovations and the births of their two sons. They'd shared anniversaries and birthdays and holidays here. She couldn't lose her home after losing her husband, but how on earth was she going to fix the business loan that needed to be paid?

"What did the bank say?" Cole's mother stood in the entrance to the kitchen. At only sixty-five, Nora was fit and tidy. She wore her hair short but stylish, with one side longer than the other.

Ruth straightened her sons' shoes into their cubbies while irritation seared her stomach. "I have thirty days to pay in full, or they'll start foreclosure proceedings."

Her mother-in-law sucked in a breath. "Oh no."

"Oh yes," Ruth countered, smothering the choice words she had for the bank.

Cole had never mentioned that he'd used their home as collateral when he borrowed all that money for equipment. Sure, she'd signed papers, but she'd never read them. She should have asked more questions. She should have dug for details.

Making her way into the kitchen, Ruth asked, "What should I fix for dinner?"

Nora shrugged. "I made a salad."

"Thank you." She squeezed her mother-in-law's shoulder but wished that Nora had taken charge of dinner duty instead of simply making a salad. Or the plate load of cookies Ruth spotted on the counter.

Maybe they should eat cookies and salad and call it good. It didn't really matter what she cooked; her youngest son had recently adopted a picky-eater attitude, making food a fight waiting to happen. Ruth was tired of battling with him to eat what had been prepared. She was tired of trying to make sense of the wreck that was her husband's business. Hers now. She'd been his only beneficiary.

If the truth were told, Ruth was just plain tired. She felt like she was juggling swirling plates atop long sticks. Something was bound to slip and crash, and the business appeared to be the first plate destined to fall and shatter.

Noticing that Nora was fidgeting with the sleeve of her gray sweater, Ruth knew something was on the woman's mind. "What is it?"

"I called my cousin Bob Harris to see if he had any ideas."

"Of Harris Industries?" Ruth squeaked. He was her mother-in-law's rich relative who purchased failing businesses or invested in promising new ones. "What did you tell him?"

"Simply that we have a momentary cash flow problem. I asked if he might want to back Cole's company."

"And?" Ruth held her breath.

Nora tipped her head and fished a piece of

paper out of her sweater pocket and handed it over. "Bob said that this sounded more like his son's level of interest. Bo lives up here."

"His son?" Ruth read the name *Bo Harris*, along with a phone number that had a downstate prefix.

Nora shrugged again. "I didn't know about this son—but then, we were never close."

Yet she'd called him for money. That took some nerve. Hadn't she just wished her mother-in-law was more of a take-charge person? "I'll call him."

"Can't hurt," Nora said.

"I suppose not." Ruth didn't have a lot of options. The cash she needed was over three times the amount Cole's life insurance policy would pay out when the insurance company finally sent the check.

She and Cole had discussed upping that life insurance, too, but had never gotten around to it. They'd never planned on a freak accident changing everything—but then, who did? Cole had been experienced in felling trees, especially the big ones, yet that last *big one* had made Ruth a widow at thirty-eight years old.

Staring at the slip of paper, Ruth wondered if this man might be interested. Surely he was rich, and maybe he'd have some ideas. She'd call Bo Harris because she didn't have a choice and time wasn't on her side.

* * *

Bo Harris ordered another soft drink as he waited for Cole Miller's widow. Finding out that Cole had been a distant relative didn't make things any easier. Meeting his widow might not be a good idea, but guilt over the recent death of his boss festered like an open sore. Add that she'd sounded desperate on the phone, and he couldn't form the words to refuse her.

Just then, an attractive woman with thick red hair entered the diner. Bo recalled the picture on Cole's desk and knew it was her. He also remembered her from the funeral—although she was much prettier up close.

Wiping his palms against his jean-clad thighs, he stood as she approached. "Ruth Miller?"

"Yes?" She froze, then smiled awkwardly as if she'd been expecting someone else. "Are you Mr. Harris?"

He extended his hand, liking the deep tone of her voice. "My father is Mr. Harris. I'm just Bo."

She took it for a firm shake. "Very well, then, Bo."

He noticed the softness first, then how easily his hand engulfed hers. She wasn't very tall. The top of her head barely reached his shoulders. "I'm sorry about Cole."

"Thank you." Her golden brown eyes clouded over.

Seeing the sadness there kicked him pretty

good. After realizing he was still holding on to her hand, he quickly let go and gestured toward the booth. "Can I order you anything?"

"Just coffee with cream." Ruth Miller slid onto the tan vinyl seat, barely making a noise. She didn't look like she weighed much either.

He motioned for the waitress, who brandished a fresh pot of brew, and waited while Ruth's cup was filled. Then he sat down, accompanied by a symphony of groans from the vinyl-covered bench seat.

"Thank you for meeting me." She leaned forward. Eager.

The desperation in her voice when she'd called had convinced him to come. "You said this had to do with investing in your husband's business. Did you know that I work there?"

"You do?" Her eyes widened. "I do the payroll, but I don't recall a Bo Harris listed. There's a Boothe—"

He nodded as he watched the color creep up her neck and flush her cheeks. "My legal name is Boothe."

"Of course." She tipped her head. "If you're a Harris, why work for us?"

Those golden eyes of hers shone with suspicion before dulling with the realization that there was no *us* for her any longer.

Bo's gut twisted tighter. "Why? Long story."

"I'm sorry." She cut him off with a raised

hand. "No need to explain, and that was rude of me to ask. It's just that when I called, I thought—"

"That I worked for my father?" Bo cut her off this time.

She sipped her coffee and nodded. Her fingernails were short and bare. No polish, not even a shiny clear coat. Nothing high maintenance there.

"I used to a while back." Another lifetime ago.

"I see."

She didn't *see*. His father didn't, either, and leaving Harris Industries had strained their relationship.

Ruth took another sip. "So, how long have you been at Miller Logging and Tree Service?"

"Six months."

She didn't have to say a word because her expressive eyes gave a lot away. She wondered if he was there the day Cole had been killed. He was not only there but was very likely the reason that huge tree had twisted. He'd give anything to replay that day, to know for certain that the fault could be transferred from his hands to simply one of those things; but in his gut, he knew.

And that's why he was here.

She sat back, disappointed. "I'm sorry to have troubled you."

"What is it that you need?" He couldn't let her go without finding out if he could help somehow. He owed her that much. No—he owed her a whole lot more.

"Eight hundred thousand dollars."

A drop in the bucket for Harris Industries, but his father had never been interested in small businesses. No doubt that's why he'd given out Bo's number. Still, that price tag was over his bank balances, unless...

"When?"

Her lips curled in disgust. "I've got thirty days, or the bank will call the loan."

Bo shook his head. "Have they offered to restructure the note?"

"Evidently, that's already been done a couple times, and Cole added our house on the line this last time."

The twisting in his gut turned into a lead ball that threatened to pull him down even farther. She faced losing her home as well. "Any life insurance?"

She nodded. "Yes, but it's not nearly enough."

Eight hundred thousand. He had it, but not at the ready. The terms of his trust fund were clear: he had to be married a year before access would be granted. At forty years old, he hadn't ever needed the money. He'd never wanted it, but faced with this situation...

Ruth let out a sigh and slid down the vinyl seat to leave. "I know, it's just too much—but thanks for your time."

He grabbed her arm to stall her. "There is a way... A shot in the dark, really, but hear me out."

Ruth waited with glassy-looking eyes, as if tears threatened to flood and fall.

He didn't handle tears well. He didn't handle a lot of things well, but this could be that one time in his life when he'd do something of real value.

Thunder pounded in his ears, making it hard to breathe, but he finally managed to choke out a plan that sounded absolutely outrageous. "We could get married."

"What?" If Ruth stared at the man across from her any harder, her eyeballs might fall out of their sockets.

He raised the work-roughened hand that had gently circled her wrist a moment ago. "Consider it a business deal. I have a trust fund that I can only tap into after being married for a year. I know how to work with banks. Between your life insurance and my savings, we should be able to throw down some of that balance owed and get an extension."

Ruth's head throbbed.

Be ye not unequally yoked together with unbelievers.

She grimaced at the scripture from 2 Corinthians that blazed through her mind. She didn't know if Bo Harris was a believer. She knew nothing about this man, other than he had a trust fund and was a distant relative of Nora's. Of Cole's, too, for that matter.

She narrowed her eyes. "What's in it for you? Access to your trust?"

He leaned back and smiled, making the sharp angles of his weathered face soften. His teeth were too perfect not to have been modified by a skilled dental team. With his shaggy light hair and unshaven face, he looked like he'd just stepped off a Viking movie set. "Consider it a way of buying into the business. Despite the financial difficulties you've mentioned, Miller Logging and Tree Service is a solid company."

Ruth let that information sink in. Was that indeed true? She used to believe Cole when he'd said it; but then, getting the letter from the bank made her question her dead husband's words.

She'd been wondering how she'd run the business by herself. She'd only ever handled light bookkeeping and payroll. She hadn't a clue in the field. All she knew was what Cole's foreman, Frank, had told her: they were running on old contracts with few new prospects. She didn't know how to drum up business. Frank knew logging, but he wasn't a forester or a salesman. Not like Cole.

She nailed Bo with a steady gaze. "What qualifications do you have?"

A confident expression of a rich man used

to getting his way took over the smile. "I have an MBA from the Ross School of Business at Michigan. My undergrad was there as well."

University of Michigan. Pricey and prestigious. Then again, he was the son of the owner of Harris Industries. He used to work for his father—so why was he working for Cole at woodcutter's pay? None of it made sense.

"Look, you don't have to answer now. Just think about it. We'd have a working relationship, is all I'm suggesting. The marriage certificate would simply satisfy the terms of the trust. Just another piece of paper."

Her mouth went dry. "Then what?"

He shrugged. "I can have my father's attorney draw up an agreement to bring me in as a partner. We can specify the marriage to be annulled once the loan is paid in a year's time."

"Will that matter? A marriage deal instead of a real one?" Ruth couldn't believe she was entertaining the idea.

Bo chuckled. "The terms of the trust weren't specific as to what kind of marriage—only that it's a legal one. It won't matter."

Marriage mattered to her. Marriage was sacred. It wasn't to be entered into lightly. The dirt covering Cole's grave was still loose. How could she remarry when she was still in love with her dead husband?

It's just a business deal.

Ruth felt sick to her stomach. Marriage was so much more than a piece of paper or a contract drawn up by an attorney. She'd had eleven good years to prove it.

After clearing her throat, she managed a rough-sounding response. "I need some time to consider your offer."

"Of course. You have my number." He stood.

She slid out of the booth and stood as well. She had a lunch meeting in half an hour that she didn't want to miss. Especially now. She needed to bounce this off two of her friends.

They'd think she'd gone insane. Maybe she had, but she wouldn't mind another pair of shoulders carrying the business load. Bo had an MBA, and that was a higher level of education than the bachelor's in forestry that Cole had earned. Could she trust Bo Harris to be a good businessman? Could she trust him with Cole's company?

She extended her hand and looked up as Bo wrapped his fingers over hers for a handshake. He was tall and lean. Angular, even. Completely different from Cole's stocky build. Bo had broad shoulders, but would they be wide enough to shoulder Miller Logging?

Her husband had hired him. Evidently, Cole hadn't known who Bo was—a rich relative looking for…what, exactly?

Too many questions and far too many thoughts

and details to fire away at the guy right now. She needed time to sort through all this and jot down the pros and cons. She hoped the trembles rocking her body couldn't be felt through her skin as she squeezed his hand. "Thank you. I'll let you know soon."

"I'll take care of the bill." He let go and left.

She watched him stop by the cashier and pay for their drinks. She glanced at the half cup of coffee grown cold, and her stomach turned. She should have eaten something for breakfast, but the morning had gotten away from her, with lunches to pack and two little boys to drop off at school.

Heading toward her car, Ruth glanced at her watch. She had plenty of time to make it to another restaurant across town where she had plans to meet two other women who were also widowed. Despite the differences in their ages, the three of them had connected immediately at a grief support meeting held by her church.

They had little in common other than losing their husbands, but they met weekly to encourage each other. Their lunches together had helped Ruth far more than the support group had, and she clung to these couple of hours like a lifeline. A safety ring keeping her afloat.

Ten minutes later, Ruth pulled into the parking lot of the Pine Wood Inn, a log cabin–style hotel with a nice café. Once parked, she spotted

Madison Williams getting out of her car. The young widow, barely out of her midtwenties, looked frazzled.

Ruth waved. "Hey, Maddie. I see that you're early too."

"Yeah, I really need this. You guys help me so much and I—" Her voice broke. She pushed her eyeglasses up with her middle finger, looked down and then had to repeat the gesture. The glasses were too big for her delicate face.

Ruth wrapped her arm around the young woman. "What is it?"

Maddie shook her head, making the tears gathered in her eyes slide down her cheeks. "Just having a day. You know how it is."

"I sure do." Ruth gave the younger woman a squeeze.

After Cole's funeral, Ruth had shifted into autopilot. She went through the motions of everyday life because she had two boys to take care of and a mother-in-law who needed her too. Add a business to save, and Ruth couldn't roll into a ball and die no matter how badly she wanted to.

The two of them entered the café and requested a table by a window overlooking the garden. It was a real vegetable garden, planted for use by the kitchen staff. At the far end, hardy-looking pumpkins stretched in the grass. They were ripe for picking, unless a killing frost got to them first and turned them to mush.

Ruth clenched her teeth, feeling akin to those pumpkins. Had she gone soft through all this, seeking someone to rescue her?

Once seated, Maddie touched her arm. "How are you?"

The truth slipped out. "Not good."

Ruth shrugged at the concern all over Maddie's face and doubted her plan to tell them everything. Would Maddie and Erica think her crazy for considering the marriage deal Bo Harris had proposed less than half an hour ago? The alternative loomed even darker.

It was only a year of her life. After that, she assumed they'd continue to work together, but it'd be strictly business. All of it, business. She had to think of it in that light.

"And here I thought I'd be the early bird." Erica Laine, close to ten years older than Ruth and married twice as long, approached the table. She glanced at Ruth and frowned. "You look terrible."

"Been feeling that way for a couple of months now."

That earned her a not-amused smirk from Erica. "Seriously, what's going on?"

Ruth looked at Maddie, who nodded for her to open up and share. Erica waited for the answer as well. The three of them had made a pact of confidentiality the first time they'd met. Ruth trusted these two ladies, so different from herself, as if she'd known them her whole life rather than only a few short weeks.

Taking a deep breath, she spilled it all. "I've mentioned my husband's business was in trouble, but I didn't know how deep the problems went until this week. The bank has called the loan, or they'll foreclose on the house, along with repossession of the business assets used for collateral."

Erica reached across the table and grabbed her hand for a comforting squeeze.

Ruth squeezed back. "Cole has a distant cousin who's interested in buying into the business. He's pretty wealthy."

"Perfect. See? God provides," Erica said.

Ruth snorted. "Don't count my blessings so fast. His money is tied up in a trust fund that he can't access until after he's married."

Erica narrowed her gaze. "So what are you saying?"

Ruth waited while the waitress approached and doled out three glasses of water along with menus. Then she rattled off the specials for the day.

After the waitress left, Erica tipped her head. "Clarify what that means."

Ruth squirmed under Erica's hard scrutiny. "It means he proposed a business deal that included marriage."

Maddie's eyes grew wide. "You're going to marry this guy?"

Ruth shrugged. "I don't know. I mean, it's my home. My mother-in-law lives there with me and my boys. And then there's the staff of Miller Logging. That's a lot of people relying on me to make the right decision."

"Sounds like you've made up your mind." Erica frowned.

"I haven't— Oh, maybe I have, but I'm scared." Ruth took a sip of her water.

Erica nodded in understanding.

"What scares you, Ruth?" Maddie whispered.

Part of the counseling at their grief support group was to verbalize emotions so they could be dealt with. What seemed obvious needed to be spelled out by vocalization. Ruth was not only scared of letting everyone down, but she also feared losing the business and the house. To do nothing would allow everything Cole had built to fizzle away into nothing. And that would be like losing him all over again.

She couldn't let that happen—not if she had the power to save it. Ruth's eyes burned with unshed tears. "I'm terrified of making the biggest mistake of my life."

Chapter Two

Sunday night, Bo disconnected the phone call with his father's attorney. The man never took a break; but then, Bo's father had a way of keeping his minions busy. Regardless, the attorney promised a contract the following day for review.

Once in Bo's hands, he'd reach out to Ruth Miller and see where she stood. He'd offer to answer any questions she might have and give her assurances of…what? That he was a good guy?

He ran his thumb and finger down the sides of his mouth. It had been three days since they'd met at the diner, and not one word from her. He gazed over the still waters of the little lake where he'd purchased frontage. He'd bought this land when he'd been engaged for real. Then he'd found out that it hadn't been real. This wasn't, either, even though an offer of marriage to Ruth Miller had seemed like the right thing to do.

Lately, he'd done his best to do "right" things, and that included reading the Bible his mother had given him. In it, Bo found that doing the right thing had a cost. Sometimes, it cost a person everything.

That truth disturbed him more than it reassured. It wasn't the cash investment that scared him but the emotional risk. Realizing his fiancée was in love with his money had messed him up pretty good. What if this "marriage" took a wrong turn and messed him up all over again?

Leaning back in a rocking chair, he heard the wooden platform he'd built this past summer creak. The sharp irony of two women agreeing to marry him for money wasn't lost on him. At least this time, it'd be a straight-up deal, both parties going in with their eyes wide open. This might defy the institution of marriage, but Bo hoped God honored his intention to do the right thing by Ruth Miller.

His father hadn't been surprised or opposed to a marriage of convenience. Of course, Robert Harris had given Bo's phone number to Nora Miller, and that's what had started this whole thing. Would Ruth take him up on his offer?

If she wanted to save her house and the logging business, she most definitely would.

Bo blew out a breath. Doing the right thing would cost a year of his life for the sake of another. Plus, he'd come out the other side owning a business he liked in a place he loved. There were worse things that could happen to a man.

The sun dipped below the tree-lined horizon, casting shimmers of orange and gold along the water. It was quiet, save for the call of a lonesome bird in the distance. Bo commiserated with that bird.

He'd learned a long time ago that loneliness could be wrestled into submission and tamed, but Bo was tired of being alone. He'd finally found his place in the world, where he fit; and yet it could all blow up in his face if Ruth knew the truth about the day her husband died.

Bo went inside now that the sun had disappeared. He shut the door of the twenty-three-foot travel trailer he'd called home for the last five years as if he could shut out the fears that crept in on him. Throwing himself onto the couch, Bo clicked on the TV to catch the local news channel.

It wasn't long before the memory of that last argument with Sheri blurred out the TV screen. He'd brought her here, offering this property as a wedding gift—as a place where they could escape the city downstate. He'd wanted to build a home where they could bring their kids. She'd laughed at him, saying he should have purchased a condo in the Bahamas or a cabin in Colorado. And that's when he knew. She didn't love him.

She loved what he could provide as an heir to Harris Industries.

Right after breaking if off with Sheri, Bo left his lucrative position and traveled. Working odd jobs along the way, he wanted to put a whole lot of distance between him and the man he'd once been. He'd landed a logging job in Alaska. It had provided a decent paycheck, so he'd stayed on for a few years.

Maybe it was the hours spent in the woods with his Finnish grandfather when he was a kid, but there was something about the smell of the forest and the feel of a chain saw slicing through wood to make a man forget his troubles. Making room for new growth, his grandfather used to say. The whole process put Bo in mind of the scripture image of God pruning His vineyard.

This past spring, feeling duly pruned, Bo had returned to the land he'd purchased on the outskirts of Pine, Michigan. It hadn't taken long to land a job with Cole Miller. Setting up camp on this fifty-four acres had been a snap. Bo hooked up his travel trailer to the well, septic and electric he'd had installed soon after buying the property.

Unfortunately, he couldn't stay here through the winter months. Winters in the Upper Peninsula were decidedly worse than the milder temps of the Inside Passage of Alaska. He'd like to store his Airstream and find an apartment in town, but he'd have to do it soon.

He closed his eyes, drifted away and then his phone rang.

"Hullo?"

"Bo Harris?" He recognized the rich, throaty voice as Ruth Miller's.

"Yeah?"

"Am I calling at a bad time?"

He shook his head to clear it. "Fine time. What can I do for you?"

"I was wondering if we could discuss the options of your offer a little more."

He felt himself smile in spite of her seriousness. "I'll have a preliminary contract in hand sometime tomorrow. Would early evening work for you?"

She didn't answer too quickly. "Ah, yeah, that should work. We could meet at the same diner."

"Grab some food too. I'll see you there at six."

"Okay."

Bo disconnected. Running his hand through his hair, that feeling of rightness he'd experienced earlier slipped into uncertainty and downright terror. This just got *real*.

Ruth Miller was going to say yes, and tomorrow she'd throw down her terms.

Rain fell and the mild temperatures from the week before had plummeted to a chilly forty-two degrees. Ruth dodged puddles in the parking lot of the diner where she'd first met Bo Harris four days ago. It had been one week since she'd received the horrible news from the bank. She had three weeks before they started foreclosure. Pulling the hood of her rain jacket closer, she dashed inside.

The warmth of the diner, along with the aroma of mashed potatoes and gravy, embraced her. She'd left two fighting boys with their grandmother after a quick meal of grilled cheese sandwiches and canned soup. Taking a deep breath, she flicked back her hood and looked around.

Bo sat in the same booth as before. He wore a simple flannel shirt over a gray T-shirt, and his shaggy hair looked damp.

Ruth gritted her teeth. Why'd he have to be so good-looking?

Just then, he caught her gaze and waved.

She swallowed hard, not liking the swirl and tumble of her belly or the guilt that seared her soul for noticing the man's attractiveness. She might be dying inside, but she wasn't dead. Squaring her shoulders, Ruth marched forward.

"Evening." He stood and extended his hand. In spite of his lumberjack appearance, Bo had the demeanor of a man used to making business deals. Big ones.

Affixing her purse strap back over her shoulder, Ruth took his hand for the briefest of hand-shakes. "Nice weather we're having."

"The best." He smiled, not the least put off by her sarcasm. "Can I take your coat?"

"No need." Ruth shimmied out of the wet raincoat and laid it over the back of the booth toward the wall. No one lingered behind her.

She sat down and pulled a leather portfolio from her purse and laid it open. The business-loan papers were nestled in the left side pocket; a lined notepad filled with notes she'd wrestled with over the weekend rested on the right.

Bo glanced at her papers filled with bullet points and questions. "Do you want to eat first or get right into it?"

She waved her hand away. "I've already eaten, but you go ahead."

His eyes widened, as if surprised she'd do so before coming here. For the first time, she noticed the color was somewhere between blue and gray. Light and icy.

He pushed a manila folder her way. "If you'd like to read this over, I'll order. Would you like something to drink?"

"I'll take a chocolate milkshake."

"That sounds pretty good." Bo flagged down the waitress, who took his order for a cheese-burger with fries and two chocolate shakes.

Ruth opened the manila folder. There were two contracts, each only a few pages, and both appeared to be straightforward. One spelled out the marriage clause for a period of a year in order for Bo to gain access to his trust fund. They'd then opt for an annulment at the end of that time upon payoff of the outstanding business loan, whereby Bo would meet the final terms of the business buy-in and become a full partner with forty-eight percent ownership. She'd retain the controlling shares at fifty-two.

That answered one of her questions. She wanted to maintain control of the business for the sake of her sons, and it appeared that Bo wasn't going to fight her for that.

The second contract was a buy-in agreement for the business. The dollar figures were left blank, as they'd have to figure those out.

She looked up. "It's pretty brief."

He shrugged. "It doesn't have to be complicated. I see you have some notes there."

Ruth held back from tossing the portfolio and gently pushed it toward him instead. "Here's the loan paperwork—and of course, my questions are noted on the right."

She watched as Bo looked through the loan documents. He took his time, and his food arrived before he'd finished, along with their milkshakes. Staring at the mound of crispy fries on Bo's plate, Ruth delayed the waitress. "I'll take an order of fries, please."

Bo pushed his plate toward her. "We can share."

"I'll wait." Ruth stirred her shake with the straw.

Even though they were having a business meeting of sorts, it felt weird. Like a really awkward date. Like she shouldn't be here. She certainly didn't want to share his food, even though her mouth watered for those greasy fries.

Bo squirted ketchup all over his. "That's quite a list of questions you have."

Ruth took a long sip of her milkshake. It was good and cold, making her head hurt. She closed her eyes.

"Brain freeze?" Bo's voice sounded way too soft.

"Yup." Ruth needed a second or two before she opened her eyes.

When she did, Bo looked at her with a mix of compassion and something darker. It was deeper than pity, as if he could feel her pain. For a moment, she simply stared back, trying to figure out how he could possibly know what her grief felt like.

"Questions?" Bo reminded her.

Ruth felt her cheeks heat. "If we do this, I don't want anyone to know about the marriage part. No one at work and certainly not my family. Not my boys. I want this to be a true business deal, and that's all anyone ever need know."

"Agreed." Bo took another bite of his burger, chewed and swallowed. "I believe we will have to go to the county courthouse in Marquette, so at least we will be out of town."

"True." Ruth nodded. Pine was too small to have a circuit court. "Can I ask you a personal question?"

He hesitated mere seconds, but the pause was long enough to make Ruth wonder why. "You may."

The waitress delivered a plate of steaming-hot french fries to the table, interrupting Ruth's question. When she'd confirmed with the waitress that neither of them needed anything more, Ruth doused her fries with salt and pepper before squeezing a glob of ketchup on the side of the plate.

Giving up on subtlety, Ruth came right out and asked, "Are you seeing anyone?"

Bo looked taken aback by the question, but humor shone from his icy eyes rather than insult. "As in, dating?"

A snarky comment hung on the tip of her tongue, but she held back from asking if there was any other meaning to the phrase. "This would be a tough one to explain if you were."

"No. I'm not seeing anyone at present, and I won't for the entire year we're, ah, married."

Ruth couldn't believe this was happening, but that was another question checked off her list.

"How much is your life insurance payout?"

"Two hundred thousand dollars." Ruth dipped a hot fry in ketchup and popped it in her mouth.

Bo nodded. "I can match that amount now. I suggest you make an appointment with the bank, explain that I'm coming on board the business, and see if we can pay half the balance down and get a twelve-month extension on the remainder. If the bank's not willing to work with us, then the other stuff is moot."

Her heart sank. "Could they refuse?"

Bo shrugged. "It wouldn't make sense for them to refuse. Foreclosures are expensive. By cutting the balance, it should be a no-brainer."

Ruth hated the idea of the life insurance going to the loan instead of a college fund she'd hoped to set up for Ethan and Owen. Miller Logging was theirs; but even so, they might want to take a different path, and she wanted to make sure they had a choice.

Bo interrupted her thoughts. "At the end of a year, I'll pay off the remaining loan balance as final buy-in."

Ruth nodded. They'd just filled in the dollar figures for those blanks. Would Cole have approved? Was that the right amount? She really should talk to their accountant. *Her* accountant now. Her stomach rolled. She'd have to tell him everything because come spring, at tax-filing time, she'd be legally married—again.

In spite of what Bo said, their marriage deal was getting *complicated*.

"This isn't at all how you imagined things turning out." Once again, his voice had softened, and those cold-colored eyes of his shone with compassion.

Ruth realized she'd been holding a ketchup-dipped french fry in midair, deep in thought. Blinking back tears that suddenly stung her eyes, she cleared her throat. "Not at all."

She shoved the whole fry into her mouth, hating the sound of defeat in her voice. Not too long ago, she'd told her brother-in-law that the eleven years spent with Cole had been the best of her life and worth the pain of his death. She'd been blessed with a good man who'd loved her. All that might be true, but she didn't feel quite so blessed today.

Empty was the description that fit her today. Ruth swallowed hard. "I'm sorry—"

"Don't be." Bo had finished his food. He crumpled his napkin and tossed it on his empty plate. "I think our first order of business is to talk to the bank."

Ruth pulled it together. "Okay. When?"

"Sooner than later, obviously. Make an appointment and let me know when, and I'll be there. We can discuss the rest of your questions then."

Just like that, this meeting was over, and Bo

appeared restless to leave. Maybe he hadn't liked her personal question after all. But then, really, a guy who looked like him and didn't date? Come on. Still, if the bank didn't agree to their plan, it wouldn't matter what her questions might be, personal or otherwise.

"I guess we're done, then. I'll text you the time." She lifted the manila folder he'd given her. "Can I keep this?"

He nodded. "Make changes as you see fit, and we'll discuss after the meeting."

"Perfect." Ruth reached for another fry. She'd finished only half of the portion on her plate.

Bo slid down the vinyl seat as if to leave, but hesitated.

Ruth waved him away. "You don't have to stay. In fact, I'd rather look this over, here—you know, by myself."

"I'll look for your text." Bo stood and tossed a twenty on the table. "For my food."

That was more than he needed to pay, but Ruth nodded. "Good night."

"Good night."

Ruth didn't watch his exit. She picked up the contract and reread each line carefully. Was it really this simple? What was she missing? Grabbing her phone, she called her accountant's office and left an urgent message that she needed to meet with him as soon as possible.

Shoving a couple more fries into her mouth,

Ruth considered her remaining questions. Her top two could be checked off with satisfaction. She'd keep control of the business, and Bo didn't mind keeping their legal union a secret. All good news.

Jotting down one more question, Ruth ate another fry. She needed to talk to Cole's foreman as well and find out what manner of man was this Boothe Harris.

Two days later, Ruth sat at Cole's desk, making one last check for anything she might need for the bank appointment. It was lunch hour, but the two crews were out working. She'd texted Bo to let him know they had an appointment at one. He'd texted back that he'd be there.

Looking around her late husband's small office, which was tucked into one end of a construction trailer, it looked as if nothing had changed. There were folded newspapers still on the corner of his desk.

Ruth closed her eyes to keep the tears at bay. She hadn't gone through his files yet. She'd been busy grieving, paying the bills and getting their accounts sorted out. If the bank agreed to Bo's suggested terms, she'd give this marriage deal a go. She had to.

Bo would use this office...

She shifted in the leather chair, causing the faint scent of Cole's aftershave to release. The spicy smell hit her hard, and it hurt. No other man could fill this chair—or take his place.

Lord, am I doing the right thing?

Ruth didn't expect an audible answer, but a gut feeling might be nice. Her accountant thought she was on the right track, even if this was an "odd arrangement," as he'd phrased it.

Closing her eyes once again, Ruth tamped down panic before it bubbled up and spilled over. She opened the bottom drawer of Cole's desk, where he kept a folder of all the maintenance records for the business equipment. Would this help? Cole took meticulous care of his equipment, kept it clean and serviced. Surely that would help prove their worth.

Miller Logging and Tree Service had started out small, but they'd grown. They leased the lot, which had included this shabby rectangle of a building, because they couldn't afford to build an office. Ruth had helped Cole refurbish the inside of the trailer years ago, soon after she'd found out she was pregnant with Ethan. They'd shared many dreams and a lot of laughter fixing this place up.

Staring at the photo of her and the boys taken only months before Cole's death, Ruth's insides doubled down into a knot. Her dreams had always been tied to Cole's. With him gone, were there any left for her?

"Hey, Ruth, I didn't know you were here."

Frank Simonson, Cole's foreman, ducked his head inside the open door. "Anything I can help you with?"

"Yes, actually there is." Ruth needed his advice, and fast—before Bo showed up.

Frank had been with Cole since he'd started out. Cole might have had the degree in forestry, but Frank had worked for logging companies all over the Upper Peninsula since high school. Nearing fifty, Frank had a wealth of experience in the field. He also had an easygoing demeanor that had complemented Cole's high-energy intensity. Frank was someone she could trust to tell her the truth.

"What can you tell me about Bo Harris?"

Frank looked surprised. "What do you want to know?"

"Your impression of the guy."

Frank shrugged. "He's good at felling trees. He's sort of serious and quiet, but smart. Intuitive. He studies the work before him instead of jumping right in. I remember Cole asking his advice a time or two. They often came into this office, and I don't really know what it was about. Cole trusted him, though. On that, I'm certain."

Ruth digested Frank's words. Had Cole shared the business's financial difficulties? Bo hadn't given her a heads-up. Why hadn't Bo shared with her that he'd talked to her husband?

"Why do you ask?"

Ruth looked Frank in the eye and decided on discretion rather than transparency. "Evidently, he's Cole's second cousin, and he will be helping me with the business side of things."

"Probably not a bad idea. I've got you covered in the field." His gaze was steady but questioning.

"Thanks, Frank. I wouldn't want it any other way." Ruth smiled. She wanted him to know that his position was safe.

He tipped his head and left to meet one of the crews that had just pulled into the yard.

Ruth watched the men gather around Frank for a moment before coming inside. Bo was one of them. He stood slightly apart from the rest. Taller too. He wore a hard hat, but his dirty-blond hair stuck out from underneath.

Bo took off his hat and pulled Frank aside.

Frank nodded, then pointed at the office trailer.

Bo headed toward her.

She watched him walk the entire way, hoping to see something—anything—that might warn her away from the path she was currently taking. She saw nothing to scare her off but nothing comforting either.

Bo ducked to enter the office. "Do you want to ride together or separately?"

"Together, I guess." Ruth wanted to know about his conversations with her husband. She lingered over the open drawer of Cole's desk. "Can you think of anything I should take other than this list of equipment? I have last year's business tax return as well."

"That should do it." He held the door. "After you."

Ruth slid the file drawer shut and stood. When she walked by Bo, he smelled like fresh air and pine. Allergic to the latter, she sneezed.

"Bless you."

"Thanks." She sniffed and grabbed a tissue from her purse. "My car or yours?"

"I'll drive."

Ruth tried to dislodge the notion that Bo had been the one driving this entire deal. What exactly had he done for his father at Harris Industries?

Heading out into the parking lot, Ruth ignored the stares of the men who had stopped to watch them. Looking at the row of parked pickup trucks, she figured the flashy new one at the end belonged to Bo and walked toward it.

"It's this one." Bo stopped by a huge black Ford F-350 that was definitely a few years older and dirtier than she'd expected. He unlocked the doors with a beep from his key fob.

They climbed inside. The interior was much cleaner than the exterior. Ruth sneezed again, and this time her eyes watered too. "Um, maybe I should meet you there."

"Why?"

Ruth rubbed her nose, but she still sneezed. "I'm allergic to pine sap. My guess is that it's on you."

After looking down at his arm, Bo stepped out of the vehicle and stripped off the fleece-lined flannel, revealing a long-sleeved waffle weave shirt that molded to his shoulders like a superhero suit. He tossed the sap-stained flannel into the capped bed, then slipped back behind the wheel and started the engine. "I had a good-sized patch of it on my sleeves."

Ruth breathed a little easier and nodded. He still smelled like the outdoors mixed with something warm and woodsy, but not strong like cologne. Maybe it was soap or his deodorant; but whatever it was, it smelled nice—and it didn't make her sneeze.

"What do you do about Christmas?"

"What do you mean?"

"No pine tree."

Ruth didn't want to think about Christmas, which was only a couple of months away. "I have an artificial tree."

"Hmm. Any pets?"

Ruth shook her head. "Nope, allergic to most of them too."

Bo remained silent the rest of the short way to the bank, and Ruth stared out the passenger window. She sensed tension in him, or maybe it was disappointment. He looked all one-with-nature, and she'd never scored high in the out-doorsy category because of her allergies. Being allergic to pine trees and their sap kept her away from the woods, and her fear of encountering poison ivy kept her feet firmly on marked paths. Or sidewalks.

When they pulled into the bank parking lot, Ruth decided she'd ask Bo about his conversations with Cole afterward. If the bank wouldn't extend the note, everything between them became null and void. Whatever advice Cole had sought out from Bo wouldn't matter. Their marriage deal wouldn't matter either.

And she'd be right back where she started.

Chapter Three

Bo wasn't surprised that the commercial lender had agreed to extend the loan for an additional fourteen months based on the fact that they'd paid nearly half of it down. When they exited the bank, Bo held the door for Ruth. She looked pretty in a long rust-colored sweater over black leggings, but she didn't look happy.

"No turning back now."

She tried to smile, but her bottom lip quivered.

He hoped she didn't cry. Tears right now would kill him.

"I want right of first refusal if you decide Miller Logging isn't to your taste and you want to sell your share." Her deep voice sounded strong, resolute.

"Of course." He didn't anticipate that happening.

He liked the job and liked the idea of becoming part owner even more. He wanted to see Cole's vision for the business come to fruition. It was a vision he could get behind and share. One he believed in.

Bo wasn't doing all this to help only Ruth, but himself too. He'd been searching for some sense of purpose for as long as he could remember.

Back in his truck, Ruth held up the manila folder he'd given her with the two contracts. "I've made some alterations to these for you to consider."

"Let's head back to the office and scan it to my attorney to finalize."

Ruth nodded. "I told Frank that you'd be helping with the business, but I didn't tell him you were buying in."

"I don't think he'll be surprised."

"Yeah, about that." Ruth turned in her seat. "Frank said that Cole asked you for business advice. Did he know you had worked for your father?"

Bo started the engine. "No. He only knew that I had an MBA along with some logging experience. He'd had hopes that I knew someone in the US Forest Service. He'd tried to get a contract with them without success. Unfortunately, I couldn't help with that."

Ruth looked confused. "Really?"

"He wanted in on the stewardship program for the Hiawatha National Forest. With the new equipment, Miller Logging could handle larger forest-management projects that could span years at a time instead of relying solely on private jobs."

"So that's what the loan was for."

"Cole believed in sound forest-management practices and so do I." He pulled out of the bank parking lot.

"But you've only worked with us for a few months. Why would you know someone in the US Forest Service?" Ruth's deep voice was soft, as if not quite buying his conviction. And again, she'd said the word *us* as if Cole were still here.

He glanced her way. "I might not have the years of experience or education Cole had, but I grew up felling trees for firewood with my grandfather. I also worked for a logging company in Ketchikan, Alaska, for over three years."

That seemed to surprise her. "Is that when you stopped working for your father?"

"No. After I left my father's business, I traveled." Bo had wandered for nearly two years. He'd camped along the way and answered to no one.

Bo concentrated on parking his truck in the vast yard of Miller Logging. "Let's see what additions you have there."

Ruth looked like she wanted to ask more, but she took the change in subject for exactly what it was—shutting the door on that part of his life.

Bo didn't want to talk about why he'd left his father's business. It was too pathetic.

He got out of his vehicle and scanned the lot. No one remained in the yard. Despite Cole's death, there was still work lined up. Bo would have to find more, though, and he'd start with Cole's contact for bidding on the national forest-management contract. Maybe they'd get another shot. He'd seek his mom's help with that, too, and see if she had any connections he might tap.

Ruth was already heading for the office trailer, her footsteps sure and quick.

He caught up to her and held the door.

"Thanks." She stepped inside.

Bo followed her into Cole's office and sat down in one of the two metal chairs in front of the desk, while she perched on the edge of the big leather office chair.

She handed over the folder.

He scanned her additions to the contract— the right of first refusal on his share was no surprise. The second item made him pause. Looking up, he asked, "What do you mean by 'included in the day-to-day business'?"

"I played a pretty light role in the past, which left me ill-prepared to run this business. I want to learn how to do it, and I want you to teach me."

"Administrative or in the field?" Bo asked.

"Administrative."

Maybe she didn't trust him to run it right. He couldn't say that he blamed her. She had her future and that of her boys to consider. "Cole told me you two were married for eleven years. What did you do before?"

"I was a dental hygienist. It's how I met Cole." Ruth smiled as if remembering. "He came in for a cleaning, asked me out and the rest is history, as they say."

"You don't want to go back to that?"

"I gave notice when I was pregnant with Ethan. I started helping Cole and let my license expire."

"I'll do what I can." Bo hadn't figured on this request. Spending time with Ruth Miller wasn't going to be easy. She'd be a constant reminder of his failure to keep her husband safe.

He leafed through their contract, seeing her neatly printed additions, and couldn't help but remember her personal question the other day. "Should we add a line about agreeing not to see other people during the upcoming year?"

Ruth snorted. "If you prefer, but I won't be dating anytime soon. No one can replace Cole."

That sobered him. "Of course not."

Ruth stood and reached for the folder. "Let's get this to your attorney. What's his email address?"

"I'll do it." Bo stood, too, and checked his watch. It was only two fifteen. "We need to apply for a marriage license. What if we drove up there now? We could get that out of the way before they close."

Ruth considered that a moment, then squared her shoulders. "Okay, let's go."

It was the same gesture he recognized from the other night. Ruth might be small, but she was mighty. He admired the strength he saw in her. Maybe more than he should.

"Do you have your birth certificate and Social Security card?" Bo asked when they were outside in the parking lot. "Mine's in my truck."

Ruth willed the tremor that shook her to subside. This is what they'd agreed to do. "It's at home. I have to check with my mother-in-law about watching the boys after school anyway. They'll be home soon. Want to follow me?"

"Lead the way."

Ruth got in her car and gripped the steering wheel before starting the engine. How was she going to explain this man to her boys without lying?

She noticed that Bo was waiting for her, so she started her car and headed for home. It wasn't far—just a few blocks the opposite direction from the bank.

When she pulled into her driveway, Nora's car was gone. Ruth just sat there, staring, until Bo pulled in beside her. His big black truck dwarfed her minivan. Again, he waited for her to make the first move.

Ruth checked her watch. School would be out soon, and Nora was probably there, waiting to pick up the boys. Ruth might get in and out before they returned home if she made it quick. Taking a deep breath, she exited the car. The air was crisp with the scent of decaying leaves that had already fallen in the yard. Ruth loved the fall, with all its vibrant colors; but this year, with the leaves ending up dry and crunchy on the ground, autumn felt like the season of death.

Right now, Ruth felt dead too. Like she moved automatically without any feeling. Numb.

After entering the house, it didn't take long for her to find her birth certificate and stuff it into her purse. Before closing the file drawer in her makeshift office space in the corner of the dining room, she grabbed Cole's death certificate as well. Just in case. Her Social Security card was safely tucked in her wallet.

She dashed out the door and climbed into the passenger side of Bo's idling truck. "Can you drive?"

Bo nodded and backed out.

"Thank you." Ruth grabbed her phone.

She texted her mother-in-law that she had to go to Marquette with Bo Harris to file some paperwork. She added that she wasn't sure when she'd be back and to please feed the boys. Ruth suggested boxed macaroni and cheese, Owen's favorite.

It was but a few seconds before Nora texted back, asking how it went with the bank.

Ruth responded that they had another year and smiled at the celebratory emoji Nora texted back. Then Nora replied that she wanted Bo to come in when they got back. She wanted to meet and thank him personally.

Ruth wanted to say no, but she hesitated. The more casually she acted about Bo, the better. She quickly texted back that she'd ask.

"Everything okay?" Bo's voice sounded low and soft.

"Just letting my mother-in-law know where I'm going." Ruth leaned her head against the seat and closed her eyes. She doubted she'd sleep, but pretending was better than making small talk with the man she was about to marry for his money. "Let me know when we get there. I'm going to nap."

He answered in some low-toned form of *yes*.

Some time later, Ruth jerked awake after the truck hit a bump. "I really fell asleep."

"You said you were."

She hadn't meant it. Ruth straightened and looked around. They were already in Marquette, turning onto Third Street, where the domed county courthouse was perched atop a mound of grassy earth flocked by flaming red bushes.

She'd slept practically the entire way. Thirty minutes of escape.

Bo parked and got out, coming around to open her door.

"Thanks." Ruth slid from the seat. Her knee gave out, and she tripped forward.

"Easy." Bo caught her, drawing her against him.

Ruth leaned into the solid warmth of his chest for a second or two. Being tucked into his arms felt nice, and she sure could use the support, but she pulled back. "I think my leg fell asleep too."

He waited while she grabbed her purse before reaching into the glove box. He pulled out what looked like a freezer bag with folded papers inside.

"That's where you keep your important papers?"

Bo shrugged. "For now, yeah."

Ruth laughed, but he didn't join her.

The occasion was too serious for joking around, but Ruth dissolved into giggles whenever she was nervous. This was one of those times. Especially since she was still trying to shake the sensation of being held by Bo, even if it had only been for a moment.

Rolling her neck from side to side, she walked up the steps with Bo by her side. "Here we go."

"Here we go." His face looked like a stone statue.

She could only guess what he might be feeling. She wanted to yell at him that this was his idea, but the lack of confidence in his face held her back. Another shot to her already-frayed nerves.

Once inside, they were directed to the county clerk's office. It didn't take long to complete the marriage application. Handing back the paperwork, Ruth asked, "Should we make an appointment now or after the waiting period? We're from Pine."

"That depends on your plans," the office worker said.

"It's just a civil union. We're not having a ceremony." Ruth spoke for Bo since he wasn't forthcoming with the information, nor any questions thus far.

"The clerk can waive the waiting period and marry you today. If you want the judge, you'll have to come back on Friday. He officiates weddings only on Fridays."

Bo looked at her. "It'll save another trip."

That was true, but Ruth panicked. "We didn't bring witnesses."

"Oh, we have some folks in the register of deeds office who'd love to witness a wedding. It's not like you two don't seem to know what you're doing."

The young woman might as well have told them they were old enough to know better. Ruth laughed again, but it sounded shrill even to her ears. She glanced at Bo.

He still didn't look like he found the humor in any of this. "It's your call."

The word *wedding* rang in her ears like a death knell. It didn't matter if they waited two days or twelve—the end result would be the same. They'd made a marriage deal in order to save her husband's legacy and her home. There was no going back.

She held her breath for one, two seconds and exhaled. "Let's do this."

That was quick. Bo signed the marriage license and then backed up so Ruth could sign as well. He watched her closely. Despite her giggles earlier, she'd been solemn through the short civil union. It was as if she were taking a dose of nasty-tasting medicine. He didn't exactly relish the fact that he was the script to fix her financial situation, but this was the best route to take. The fastest one too.

She looked up at him and smiled. It was a brave-up sort of expression, as if she'd given herself a pep talk and was trying to make the best of it.

He couldn't think of a single thing to say that might ease the lines of worry around her perfectly shaped lips. "Want to get something to eat?"

Her brow furrowed, and she glanced at her watch. "Ah, I, yeah, that'd be good. I didn't eat lunch."

"Me neither." His stomach growled.

Ruth laughed—a rich sound instead of the edgy giggles he'd heard before. "I guess not."

He chuckled, too, and held open the door for her, inhaling her soft scent as she passed. Subtle, like the clean smell of thick pine needles strewn on the forest floor.

Bo slammed the brakes on that train of thought. He had no business noticing how she smelled or looked, or how nice she'd felt against him—especially how nice she'd felt in his arms. They'd done what they had to do. He'd show her what he could about owning a business, and they would run it together. Strictly business. That's all they'd be. It's what he'd promised.

"What are you in the mood for?"

Her deep voice cut through his thoughts. "What?"

"Pizza, burgers, pasta?" Ruth checked them off on her fingers.

Of course, she was talking about food. "There's a place within walking distance that has a varied menu. I remember having good food there earlier this year."

"I rarely come to Marquette, so I'm in your hands."

Blocking any thoughts that comment stirred,

Bo quickly explained, "I've always liked this college town. Good restaurants."

Ruth walked in step with him. "Have you been here often?"

"A few times." He'd played the tourist after he'd moved back to Michigan, and he'd been here before on business for his father.

"Oh."

They walked the remaining couple of blocks in silence. The day was cool but sunny, and Bo enjoyed the view of the Lake Superior waterfront with a long breakwall in the distance. At the restaurant, Bo opened the door for Ruth.

"You don't have to keep doing that."

"It's habit." One he'd learned from his grandfather but had served him well working for his father. The women he'd worked with had loved the small gesture. Not so with Ruth.

They'd already been seated and given menus and water when he noticed that she looked nervous. "What's the matter?"

"This place is too nice."

"It's casual." He might be pushing the business casual dress code with his long-sleeved T-shirt, jeans and work boots, but Ruth looked perfect in her autumn-toned sweater and leggings.

Focusing on the menu before his gaze wandered, he added, "Besides, we just sealed our business deal."

"What did you do when you worked for Harris Industries?"

He looked up at the slight edge in her voice and caught the narrowing of her eyes. Would she believe that he'd experienced one too many hostile takeovers? "Acquisitions and mergers."

Her eyes grew round as gold dollars; but then she smiled, if ever so slightly. "That makes sense—although I can't picture you in a suit. It's the shaggy hair."

"I kept it short then." It had been a royal pain keeping up with those hair appointments. Not anymore. Still, he got the feeling her term *shaggy* wasn't a compliment.

"So Miller Logging must be small potatoes comparatively."

True, but Bo shrugged. "I know potential when I see it."

"Did Cole show you the books?"

"No." But he'd heard enough to know that they needed to land more profitable contracts, and soon.

Ruth shook her head. "I just don't get it. Cole never told me the reason for the bigger equipment, not his goals for the business and especially not the past-due loan. Why would he keep that from me?"

"Maybe he didn't want you to worry."

"Did he tell you that?"

"No, but it makes sense. Cole once told me

that he wanted to leave something good behind for his boys. Something they could take pride in." The minute he saw tears gather in Ruth's eyes, Bo wished he hadn't repeated those words.

"Cole was a good man, Ruth. There's nothing he had to hide."

She nodded, but a few of those tears leaked out and ran down her cheeks.

Feeling like a heel, he reached out and covered her hand with his with an awkward pat. "I'm sorry to have upset you."

She surprised him by gripping his hand and squeezing hard. "You haven't. In fact, you've helped more than is imaginable."

He pulled his hand away. She wouldn't think so if she knew he might be responsible for her husband's death. "Look, I'm doing this for me too. It's a good investment."

"Right." She studied the menu.

Great. He'd either embarrassed her or hurt her feelings. And he'd made a bad move choosing this cozy restaurant, which was more suited for a date than just grabbing a bite to eat. He perused his menu and set it down. He wanted pasta. There was nothing he could do about the weirdness of the day. The whole situation was uncomfortable on more than one level, but he was doing his best not to let it interfere with dinner.

The waitress came for their orders. Ruth

chose a hefty salad with blackened tuna that sounded pretty good, but he still ordered the ravioli.

Waiting for their food was agony. Ruth had clammed up, and Bo didn't have a clue how to get her talking again. By the time their dinners arrived, he was of the mind to get it all boxed up to go, but that would be stupid. They'd come here to eat.

The spicy aroma of the marinara-covered ravioli enveloped him. He was just about to dig in when he noticed that Ruth had bowed her head. Was she praying? Seeing her lips move answered that question.

"Maybe you could say a blessing for both of us," he whispered.

Ruth's head came up quick and her big eyes grew even larger. "You pray?"

"Not like I should."

Her mouth dropped open and then closed before she asked, "So you believe in God and salvation through Christ?"

"Yes."

He thought he spotted a glimmer of fear flash in those golden eyes before she dropped her head again, this time softly murmuring a mealtime prayer.

"Amen." After dipping a piece of warm bread into the sauce, Bo dug in.

"Can I ask you something?" Ruth's voice was whisper soft.

"Sure." He braced for it.

"Did you go to Cole's funeral? I don't remember seeing you."

"I stayed in the back and left right after." He'd been a coward who couldn't face her to pay his respects.

"Oh."

He wasn't sure if she believed him, but there was nothing he could do about it now. He made quick work of his meal while Ruth did little damage to her big salad. He knew better than to ask but did it anyway. "Something wrong?"

She scrunched her nose. "Why didn't you say anything about your faith before?"

"Like at the diner?" Of all the things that might bother her, she chose this?

Ruth nodded.

He shrugged. "Some things are better left out of a business conversation."

"How is your faith one of those things?"

"I wanted you to weigh my words by their own merit." Bo didn't want to sway her by professing his faith or make her think he was trying to manipulate her.

She considered what he said closely, as if trying to read between verbal lines. Finally, she shrugged. "Okay."

It made him chuckle as he continued eating.

By the time he was done, she'd eaten a little more and pushed her plate away.

Ruth raised her hand for the waitress. "I'd like a take-home box, and we'll need separate checks."

The waitress grabbed his empty plate and dashed away.

"I planned on picking up the tab."

Ruth gave him a stern look. "I'm paying my own way. We're business partners, and I prefer not to get into an *I'll-get-this-one-and-you-get-the-next* sort of thing."

He couldn't argue with that. They may be legally married, but they were far from wed. He couldn't even claim friendship at this point. "That's fine."

She gave him a pert nod, pulled her wallet from the depths of her gigantic purse and slapped a credit card on the table. "Good."

He felt the corners of his mouth twitch at her tone, as if she'd shown him who was boss.

"What's so funny?" She'd caught him.

"Not a thing." He couldn't very well explain that he found her spunk as attractive as it was amusing.

She glared at him.

He raised his hands in surrender. "Sorry, it's been a long day."

She gave him a contrite smile. "Yes. It has been."

Fortunately, the waitress saved the day by arriving with their respective bills and a box for Ruth's leftovers. She left with their plastic and returned soon after. This awkward deal-sealing dinner was finally over.

The walk back to his truck was a silent one. By the time they got there, Bo didn't bother holding the passenger door open for Ruth. This time, he simply unlocked the doors with a press of a button on his key fob. When they were both inside and buckled in, he started the engine and headed back to Pine.

It didn't take long for the silence to become deafening. He glanced at Ruth. She looked lost, like a pup dumped on the side of the road.

"Are you okay?" he asked as gently as he could.

"No, I'm not. This is unbelievable, and yet I don't know what else I could have done."

"It's the right thing to do, all things considered."

She looked at him then. "Why doesn't it feel right?"

He reached out his hand, surprised when she took it. "It's going to be okay." Bo gently squeezed before letting go.

"I hope you're right."

He hoped so too. And he kept hoping the whole way back to the Miller house. When he pulled into her driveway, he shifted into Park and waited for her to exit his truck.

"Could you come in for a minute? Nora would like to meet you."

He tipped his head. "Nora?"

"Cole's mother. She's the one who called your father, her cousin."

He looked at the house with the soft glow of lights in the windows. The sun had just set, and dusk was closing in on them. He'd meet them sometime, he supposed; might as well be now.

"Sure." He turned off the engine and got out.

Just then, the side door opened with a bang, and two little boys with varying shades of red hair like their mother's came running out.

"Mom!" The littlest one ran the fastest and threw himself into her opened arms.

The older boy eyed him suspiciously. "Who are you?"

"Boys, this is Mr. Harris, your dad's cousin. He's going to help with the business." Ruth turned, her hands on the shoulders of the youngest boy. "This here is Owen, and his older brother, Ethan."

"Nice to meet you both." Bo smiled even though he felt as if he'd just been hit by lightning. The burn was that sharp and quick.

In the eyes of those two boys, Bo recognized the stark expression of loss. They'd not only lost their dad but also their road map to becoming a man. Bo knew that sharpness of loss when his grandfather died. He'd been on the edge of his teens, older than these two, but the pain of grief didn't respect a tender age.

Bo suddenly saw himself in the two pairs of eyes staring at him, and it hurt pretty good. The enormity of costing these two kids their father sliced through him, and this marriage deal twisted into a new direction. He'd wanted to help Ruth, but her boys would need help too.

Marrying Ruth had been a way to save the business and ultimately buy into it; but suddenly, that year-long contract stretched further out into the future. Becoming part owner of Miller Logging came with more responsibility than he'd bargained for. Doing right by Cole meant taking care of his entire family, no matter the cost.

Chapter Four

"Are you a lumberjack like my dad?" The littlest one stared at him with big dark gray eyes.

The older boy scoffed. "Don't be stupid."

"Ethan!" Ruth's cheeks were rosy.

Bo stifled a laugh, then turned serious eyes upon the older boy. "I'm not near as good as your dad."

Ethan had eyes like his mom—golden with dark brown around the iris. Those eyes glared at him now.

"Ethan, Owen—inside." Ruth corralled both boys and pushed them toward the front door of the house. "Mr. Harris is here to meet your grandma."

"Your grandmother and my father are cousins," Bo explained.

"Are you our uncle?" Owen asked.

Bo smiled at the boy. "No, just a distant cousin."

The youngster smiled back, his expression sweet.

Ethan grumbled under his breath but followed them inside.

Bo noticed that the house had the welcoming feel of a real home. It was older than most, smack-dab in the middle of town. It might have been one of the first built. The rooms were large, with hardwood floors and crown molding along the ceilings. He followed Ruth and her boys into the kitchen, where a smallish woman in her sixties was making tea.

"Nora, this is Boothe Harris."

Hearing his given name pronounced by Ruth made it sound better somehow.

"How do you do, Boothe." Nora Miller offered her hand.

Hearing his father's cousin say it didn't have the same impact, which was probably a good thing. He took her offered hand. "I go by Bo."

"Oh." Ruth's mother-in-law looked confused.

"My legal name is on the payroll." Bo felt like he needed to explain why Ruth might have used his given name. Maybe *Boothe* had gotten stuck in her mind from the civil ceremony at the county clerk's office earlier that afternoon.

"Would you like something to drink, Bo?" Nora asked.

He wasn't sure he should stay, so he glanced at Ruth.

"We have cookies too. Have a seat." Ruth pulled out a chair at the table.

"Oh, Ruth, take him into the living room, where he can be more comfortable."

"No, this is fine. I can't stay." Bo didn't want to stay. Today had been awkward enough. Still, it wasn't like he had anyone or anything waiting for him at the camper, other than perusing the apartment ads in the local paper.

Owen climbed into the chair next to him, knelt on the seat and leaned toward him with his elbows on the table. "I thought a booth was at the diner?"

Bo thought the little guy resembled Cole. "Yes, but it's also a name."

"I never heard it before." Ethan slid into the chair opposite him.

Bo couldn't decide if the older boy was plain ornery or making his position as man of the house known. "I'm named after my grandfather, Kalle Boothe Tervonen."

Owen's eyes widened at the foreign-sounding name, while his older brother's narrowed.

"That sounds Finnish." Nora set a plate of thick and chewy-looking chocolate chip cookies in front of him, along with some napkins.

"It is. Both of my mother's parents emigrated from Finland to the Keweenaw Peninsula." Bo reached for a cookie.

"Is your family still there?" Nora asked.

"Just my mom. She lives in Toivola."

"What's your favorite cookie?" Owen was on to another subject.

"Anything homemade."

"You'll like these, then. Nora is a fabulous baker. Milk?" Ruth asked.

"Please."

"You are, too, dear." Nora slipped into the seat on the other side of him. "How is your father? I haven't seen him in ages."

"Me neither." That truth slipped out. "I've been traveling some."

"Oh?"

"Bo worked with a logging company in Alaska these last three years." Ruth bent to set the glass of milk in front of him.

Her hair brushed the side of his face. Again, he caught the subtle scent of her. Yeah…she smelled good.

Ruth stepped back quickly as if she'd heard his thoughts. She didn't sit down and instead moved around the kitchen, wiping counters with a dishcloth. Then she filled a teakettle with water and placed it over a gas flame on the stove.

"Did you see grizzle bears?" Owen's questions kept coming, distracting him from Ruth.

Again, he chuckled, especially at the kid's mispronunciation. "Not where I lived, but I saw some grizzlies farther north of Juneau."

Ethan stared him down. "I saw a bear in town once."

"Black?" Bo believed him. There were black bears in Northern Michigan, both the lower and upper.

The boy nodded.

"When did you see a bear in town?" Ruth quizzed her son.

"With Dad, when we went to the transfer station." The boy made it sound as if it had been yesterday.

Bo spotted sadness in Ruth's eyes, and his gut twisted.

"Do you like bears?" Owen asked.

"Yes, I do." He'd gone on a bear hunt with his father once, along with a couple of clients. It wasn't something he'd care to repeat. He thought it more sporting to track an animal rather than bait it, but he wasn't much of a hunter. He preferred to fish.

"Let Mr. Harris eat his cookies, Owen," Ruth called from behind him.

Why'd she stay in the kitchen? Bo nearly cringed at the formality of being called *Mister*, not to mention three sets of eyes watching his every move, between Ruth's boys and her mother-in-law.

He washed down the last of his cookie with a long swig of milk and stood. "It's late. I'd better go. Nice to meet you all."

"Are you coming back?" Owen slipped off his chair to stand, too, as if ready to follow.

Ethan's eyes merely challenged him. He had to give the kid credit for posing as Ruth's protector.

"I'm sure he will. Owen, help Grandma take those dishes to the sink," Ruth said, then to him, "I'll walk you out."

"Bye, Bo," Ruth's mother-in-law added as she herded Owen back to the table.

He nodded and left with Ruth at his heels.

Once outside, he turned around. Ruth stood on the side stoop, and her feet were bare. He didn't know when she'd taken off her boots, but she'd seemed jumpy ever since they'd arrived. She could have changed her whole outfit, considering that she hadn't been around the kitchen table while he was seated.

"You're going to catch cold." He hadn't meant to sound irritated.

"I'm fine." She waved his concern away with one hand. "Listen, I'll be in the office tomorrow after I drop the boys off at school—you know, to start learning."

"I'll see what Frank has lined up." Bo hoped it was a big job requiring his help. He didn't relish the task of teaching Ruth about business. It would mean hours spent together.

"We should tell Frank about your buy-in. He probably needs to know."

"Yes." He looked at her bare feet, which were slim and pretty.

He'd never thought of feet as *pretty* before, but hers were. She didn't wear any polish like Sheri used to. No bright red or hot pink colors; instead, Ruth had a small tattoo of a trio of stars above her pinkie toe.

He stared at that black ink on her skin before finally glancing up. "Good night."

Ruth looked like she wanted to say more, but she didn't. "'Night."

He climbed in his truck and noticed that Ruth hadn't gone inside. She stood watching as he backed out. What did she hope to see?

Driving away from town and into the darkness, responsibility for the Miller family seared his insides. He considered Ruth's two boys and wanted to do right by them. That meant more than keeping Miller Logging solvent enough for them to one day take over. It might mean a lot more.

Could he reach out to those two boys? Ethan didn't trust him. And neither did Ruth. He'd have to remedy that, starting tomorrow.

"He seemed overwhelmed." Nora set her empty teacup in the sink, then turned around to lean against the counter.

"Maybe he's not used to kids." Ruth shrugged.

She'd noticed tension in him as well; but then, it had been an overwhelming day for both of them.

"Perhaps you're right. He seems nice, though. And handsome."

"Yes." What else could Ruth say?

"So, he's going to help you with Cole's company?"

"Yes." Hearing her mother-in-law label the business as Cole's sliced through her. "Bo is buying in as a partner. It was the only way to save the house."

Nora nodded as if considering that information. "You're a modern-day Ruth, in a way."

"What?"

"You know, the book of Ruth in the Bible."

"Yes, of course."

Nora smiled. "Well, Bo might be your Boaz, a kinsman redeemer come to save us from ruin."

Ruth laughed—it was better than crying—because there was too much truth in her mother-in-law's words. "And if you're my Naomi, don't bother telling me to sleep at his feet."

Nora laughed, too, but then turned serious. "You're doing a good thing, Ruth. Cole would have wanted Miller Logging and Tree Service to go on."

"I know. He wanted the boys to follow in his footsteps, I think. Family business and all that."

"The boys may choose differently when they're grown, but at least they'll have options.

They will know you had their futures in mind by saving their father's business." Nora's eyes were filling with tears.

Ruth looked away in hopes of keeping her own tears at bay. Could she really keep her husband's legacy alive that long?

Nora touched her shoulder, giving her a long look. "Cole would want you to go on too."

Ruth searched her mother-in-law's gaze. What exactly did she mean by that? Of course she'd go on living, but Ruth didn't think that's quite what Nora meant. She didn't want to go there—not one bit. "It's too soon."

"Of course it is now, but maybe in time." She patted her shoulder. "Bo Harris must have considerable resources."

Ruth snorted. Nora had no idea how she'd legally tapped those resources. Ruth hoped her mother-in-law would never know. It might hurt her to know. Besides, after a year, she and Bo would get that annulment and be nothing more than business partners.

Her mother-in-law's concerned gaze still rested on her. "You never know… In time, after working together, you might think differently."

Ruth's mouth fell open. Was she really pushing Bo toward her like Naomi had pushed Boaz? This wasn't a Bible story—this was the here and now.

Nora smiled. "Okay, maybe I'm getting ahead

of myself. I just want you to know that finding love again is what I hope for you."

Ruth didn't know what to say to that, so she hugged Nora, hoping to end this little rabbit trail. "You'll stay with me?"

Her mother-in-law hugged her back. "Of course."

Ruth would never leave Cole's mother. And like her biblical namesake, where Ruth went, Nora would always be welcome to go too. Plain and simple. She let go when she heard the boys arguing in the other room.

"I'll go to them. Relax, you look like you've had a long day."

Ruth watched her go into the family room and listened as Nora intervened in whatever toy was being fought over. It was nearing the boys' bedtime anyway. Time to put away the toys.

She yawned.

Her bedtime wasn't far off, either, but she didn't look forward to climbing into her large bed. After two months, she might be used to sleeping alone, but it didn't mean she liked it. She even missed Cole's soft snore.

"Mom…" Ethan's raised voice came closer.

Ruth braced for impact. What now?

Her oldest came into the kitchen. "Owen took my fidget spinner."

"You have more than one."

".Yeah, but they're mine." He looked so frustrated, her eight-year-old son.

Why Ethan hoarded them away from Owen, Ruth didn't understand. She was too tired to find out as well, so she ruffled her son's hair. "It's time for bed. I'll find your spinner tomorrow. Get your pajamas on, and brush your teeth. I'll be up in a minute."

Ethan's shoulders slumped as he walked away. Her brave boy was an angry one lately, but she knew that he loved his little brother, even if he didn't always show it.

Both her sons were trying to deal with the permanent absence of their dad in their own ways. Owen had stopped talking right after Cole's death, and Ethan had stepped up to help, but nothing had worked.

It wasn't until after their uncle Cash, Cole's younger brother, had taken the boys for a summer trip to a cabin in the woods that Owen's tongue had been unleashed. Cash had had help from a woman he'd grown up with and fallen hard for. Monica had recently been diagnosed with cancer and was getting treatment.

Ruth wasn't the only one suffering. There was plenty of pain all around these days. Ruth needed to remember that, just like she needed a reminder that God was with her. Even if she didn't *feel* like God was near, the scriptures promised that He'd never forsake her.

Ruth hung her head and uttered a quick prayer. She prayed for Monica and for Maddie and Erica. She prayed for her boys and for Nora too. Her mother-in-law had lost her husband ages ago, and now one of her two sons— yet she had hopes for Ruth to find love again. Dear Nora.

Naomi from the Bible had orchestrated Ruth's meeting with Boaz just like Nora had been the instigator in Ruth calling Bo. Like that story in the Bible, Bo had saved them from financial ruin with marriage. But that's where the comparison stopped.

Ruth wasn't interested in finding love with anyone, let alone a man she'd agreed to marry for his money. Ick, she'd actually married a man for his money!

Bowing her head, she said a quick prayer for Boothe Harris, asking God to protect him. Actually, to protect them both.

The next morning, Bo pulled into the parking lot at work. He kept his truck running while he waited for the foreman to arrive. Seven thirty might be early for the eight o'clock start time, but he wanted to give Frank a heads-up before Ruth arrived. Whenever that might be. Not to mention that he didn't have keys to the office. He'd remedy that today.

The sun hadn't yet risen, but the eastern sky

brightened with the promise of a clear day. October weather in the Upper Peninsula ran the gamut between warm, rainy and cold enough to snow, but today's forecast was seasonably cool and sunny. Perfect fall weather. Too bad he'd be stuck inside the office.

Bo spotted Frank's truck pulling in, so he cut the engine and got out.

"Morning. You're here early."

Bo nodded. "Yeah, about that. Ruth's coming in today."

Frank tipped his head.

"She wants to learn the administrative side and wants me to teach her," Bo added.

Frank didn't look surprised. "Good thing it's a light day. We have a few tree removals, trimming and several firewood deliveries. I won't need you."

"Good." Bo followed Frank to the office trailer.

Once inside, Frank flipped on the lights. "Want coffee?"

"Thanks, I'll make it." Bo headed straight for the counter in the corner with a sink and made the first pot.

It was chilly inside the trailer, so when he spotted the thermostat, he clicked it up a couple of notches to warm the place up before Ruth arrived.

"Morning. That smells good. Is the coffee ready?"

Bo turned at the sound of Ruth's rich voice. "Not yet."

"Frank, do you have a minute? There's something you should know."

Bo waited for Frank to follow Ruth into Cole's office before joining them.

Frank glanced at him and then focused on Ruth. "What's up?"

"I have asked Bo to help me run things, and he's buying into the business. I still have the controlling share of Miller Logging and Tree Service, but going forward—" Ruth gestured toward Bo "—we'll be working as partners."

Without really saying it, Ruth had just informed Frank that Bo was the new boss.

Frank looked at him and then back to Ruth. "Makes sense."

Bo let out the breath he'd been holding. Frank was a good guy, but he didn't know. He couldn't have known about Bo's carelessness the day Cole had died. Bo would never forget how Frank had patted his shoulder after the first responders had arrived. Frank had said that he'd done everything he could, but Bo knew that wasn't true. He could have done more, been more careful.

Bo rubbed the back of his neck. "I'll be figuring out the office today, I guess."

"See you later." Frank chuckled and left.

Ruth followed but didn't leave. Bo could hear her rustling around the kitchen area.

Bo scanned the cramped office space and the piles of who-knew-what that lay stacked on the desk. Cole had been unorganized when it came to paperwork. Bo had joined him in this office enough times to know that Ruth's husband didn't care for the mundane side of running things. He had been great in the field, even better at sales, but—

"Coffee's ready. Do you want a cup?" Ruth held two steaming mugs in each hand and offered him one. "I don't know how you take yours."

Bo reached for it. "Black is fine."

Ruth didn't let go. "Is that how you drink it?"

He looked into her earnest face and those golden eyes. "I like a little cream."

"Same as me." She smiled and handed over the other mug. Then she darted back to the tiny kitchenette.

He took a sip.

Ruth had returned. She watched him, waiting.

And then it dawned on him. "Thank you."

"You're welcome." Again with the bright smile, as if she was forcibly putting on a positive face.

This was going to be a long day.

"Where should we start?" Ruth sounded much too chipper.

"We need to go through the stacks of paper and figure out what they are for." Bo sat in the metal chair, leaving the big leather office chair for Ruth.

"Wouldn't you be more comfortable over there?" She offered him the leather one.

Bo would be more comfortable doing this on his own, but that wasn't going to happen. Ruth was here with her game face on, ready to dig through her dead husband's papers for what might be the first time.

Without a word, he got up and sat in the leather chair. Reaching for the closest stack, Bo noticed the invoices stamped "paid," with what looked like bank receipts stapled to them. "Who billed your customers?"

"I did. Cole gave me a list of clients and their cost for services every week. I'd mail them a bill with a return envelope. The checks came here. Some of them didn't always pay on time, but…" Ruth shrugged.

Bo pinched the bridge of his nose. "We need to automate."

"I kept a spreadsheet. We'd balance the books every month. It worked."

Bo gestured to the stacks of papers. "All this can be done electronically, and anyone who doesn't pay within thirty days should be charged a late fee."

Ruth grimaced. "I don't think that will go over well. This is a small town."

"Look at it this way. They'll get a discount if paid within thirty days. After that, the price is a little higher. After sixty days, higher still. See what I mean?"

Ruth nodded. "Incentivize them to pay early."

"Yes." He looked around. "Computer?"

"I have Cole's laptop at home. I didn't think to bring it with me."

"You can bring it tomorrow. Today, why don't we go through everything, file what we need and toss what we don't. Then we can look at what you turned in to your accountant."

Ruth nodded again, but she looked uneasy.

It hit him again that this might be hard on her—going through her husband's work. "Are you up for it?"

"I've put it off too long as it is. Let's do this."

Bo smiled. She'd said the same thing yesterday when they'd gone to the courthouse.

Ruth was no quitter, and she was willing to learn. Two things that were often lacking in the personnel he'd encountered in many of the acquisitions and mergers he'd overseen while working for his father.

This "merger" would definitely prove interesting. Not only did he wish to fulfill the original owner's vision for the company, but he'd also gone into this with the intent to stay. Running a business on his own might be new ground for him, but he looked forward to the challenge.

But then, he wasn't alone.

Glancing at Ruth's solemn face, the enormity of the year ahead settled on his shoulders. Miller Logging and Tree Service had to not only go on but also prosper for the sake of the Miller family. No matter how difficult it might be working with Ruth, he'd give her his best.

And this time, he wouldn't fail.

Chapter Five

By lunchtime, Ruth needed a break from organizing. She'd found a contact name and number for the Forest Service in Cole's desk and given it to Bo. He'd promised to reach out to the guy.

She sat at the desk, watching as Bo jammed a whole lot of paper into a garbage bag. Paper with her husband's handwriting on it, scraps of notes and lists—all of it had been Cole's. Thoughts that had most likely been jotted down before he forgot. She used to find sticky notes at home too.

Her heart ached.

"I think I'm going to run home for lunch," Ruth announced.

"What would you like me to do with this?" Bo lifted a desk-sized calendar pad that they'd leaned against the wall.

"I'll take it home. The boys will enjoy it." Ruth smiled to keep from crying.

Cole had always been a doodler while on the

phone. Seeing his notes, his desk calendar with all his funny-faced scribbles, swamped her. When would it get easier? When would she stop feeling as if she were peering over the edge of a cliff?

Bo's cell phone rang. "Excuse me while I take this."

"Sure." Her curiosity sharpened when he exited the tiny office.

Through Cole's office window, Ruth watched the frown on Bo's face deepen. Whoever it was bore bad news. Whoever it was, was none of her business.

She grabbed the calendar pad and stepped out into the open area of the office trailer to fetch her jacket from the hook near the door.

"Hmm. Let me know if another apartment opens up." He turned, saw her and gave her a wave while he dialed another number.

She fumbled the calendar.

Bo stepped forward to help her.

"I have it." Ruth slipped her purse over her shoulder and tucked the calendar under her other arm. It might be none of her business, but she couldn't seem to stop herself. "Are you looking for an apartment?"

His eyebrows lifted.

"Sorry, I heard you just now."

"For the winter months. Do you know of any temporary places? Month-to-month?"

"No, but I have an apartment above our garage that is not being used."

"Thank you, but I'll find something."

Her hackles went up. "It's a nice little studio. Cole and I lived there while we renovated the house. My brother-in-law stays there when he's on leave—"

"All the more reason I can't take it." His eyes were an icy gray, and he didn't look like he'd budge.

Ruth gave him a pointed look for interrupting. "What I was going to say is that my brother-in-law won't be home for at least eight to ten months, so there's your winter time frame."

He stared at her.

She stared back.

Part of her wanted Bo where she could keep an eye on him. Another part of her felt like she owed it to him because he'd plunked down a huge chunk of change on that loan. Without him stepping in, she'd have lost her home, garage apartment and all.

"I'll think about it." He gave her the slightest of smiles.

"Where are you living now?" Oh, why'd she keep asking questions?

"About ten miles east of here, I own some land where I have a camper."

She remembered the pop-up camper that Cole had finally sold because he didn't have time to fix the leaks. They'd gone on a couple of camping trips with it. The boys had been snuggled in on one end in a foldout bed, and she and Cole were in another. Remembering the good times they'd had, she could practically smell the musty odor of the canvas.

Coming back to the here and now, Ruth didn't picture Bo as a pop-up kind of guy. "How big is it?"

"Twenty-three-foot travel trailer."

Not small, but certainly not one of those ginormous fifth-wheels either. Campers, no matter how fancy, were not meant for winter use in the central UP.

A vision of Bo huddled around a campfire took front and center in her mind, making her want to push the apartment even more. "The nights are getting cold."

"I have heat."

"What if it snows?" It wasn't uncommon for the first measurable snow to fall in October. Pine had received nearly two hundred inches of snow last winter. Bo had maybe a month before the snow that fell stayed.

"I'll figure it out." His jaw tightened.

Ruth opened her mouth and then shut it. She'd pushed enough. This was his problem, and she had enough of her own. "I'm grabbing lunch. Do you want me to bring you anything?"

"I'm good. Thank you." He took a few steps

toward her. "I assume your boys will be home in a couple hours. We can finish up tomorrow."

Ruth glanced out the window. Frank and a crew had just pulled in, and Bo looked antsy to meet them. Obviously, he'd had his fill of organizing too. If the truth were told, Ruth didn't want to come back. Not today. "That would be fine."

Bo opened the door for her so she wouldn't have to put down the bulky calendar pad.

"Do you have an address?"

He held the door, looking impatient for her to leave. "I use a post office box in town."

"Oh." Well, that was a bucketload of information. Did he think she'd stalk him if she knew where he lived? Ruth chuckled. Maybe she would. Hadn't she wanted to keep an eye on him? "See you tomorrow. I won't forget the laptop."

"Tomorrow." He gave her a dismissive nod.

Ruth made her way out and into her car.

Frank had told her that Bo was quiet, but Ruth thought him very closed. Measured, even, like he said only what he needed to and nothing more. All the more reason to get him to take the apartment over her garage.

If she was going to run a business with the guy, she needed him to open up a little so she could at least get to know what he was all about. How else could she learn to trust him as a partner if he never shared his thoughts? Never shared anything about himself?

Ruth tossed the calendar in the back seat of her minivan, then slid behind the wheel. She wasn't sure what to expect from Bo. He seemed to know what he was doing, but what if that wasn't quite true? Ruth certainly didn't need any more surprises in her life.

"How'd it go?" Frank had come inside to grab his lunch from the fridge.

"I see where we can improve on some things. Automate in areas." Bo had seen more than he'd wanted, namely watching Ruth trying to hold it together as they went through her husband's desk.

Ruth was completely different from Sheri in that she hid her feelings. Or tried to. Ruth did her best to keep it together. She didn't let the whole world know she was upset like Sheri used to. He often wondered what he'd seen in his ex-fiancée.

"Cole wasn't much for computers," Frank said. "He did everything from his phone."

Bo nodded in agreement. "That's an understatement."

He needed to ask Ruth about that phone and see what business-related items were on there. Cole's methods were old-school. He had built his business primarily from word of mouth. It was ripe for growth, and Bo looked forward to taking it to the next level, starting with a website that had the ability to receive estimate requests from potential customers.

"What's the next job?" Bo asked.

"Firewood deliveries for the rest of the afternoon. I'm joining Josh to take down a residential tree."

"Need help?" Bo wouldn't mind spending the rest of the day out of doors.

"We got it. Use your expertise to save this business." Frank slapped him on the back and left.

Bo's responsibility was making sure everyone continued to receive a paycheck, including Cole's widow. He couldn't let them down. He wouldn't. Pulling the scrap of paper Ruth had given him from his jeans pocket, Bo read the contact name and number for the Hiawatha National Forest stewardship coordinator. It was a long shot, but grabbing his phone, Bo called his mother.

"Boothe, what a nice surprise. Everything okay?"

"Everything's fine." Not the most truthful answer but the correct one. He rarely called his mom in the middle of a workday, so he'd expected the concern in her voice. "Quick question. Didn't you once tell me that a friend of yours had a son who was a forester somewhere? Do you know if he works around here?"

"Hmm, can't think of anyone off the top of my head. Oh, now, just a moment. I think Janet's son recently hired on in Gladstone. She was just telling me about it. I can't remember which one of her boys it was."

Bo smiled. It wouldn't be the same guy, but Gladstone was the location of a Hiawatha National Forest supervisor's office. Also home to the coordinator. "Can you get me his name?"

"I have a better idea. Come up this weekend, and we can both find out."

"Sorry, Mom, this weekend I'm working." He still had a lot of paperwork to go through in order to form a solid business plan.

"Aw, that's too bad. Hey, the church is celebrating Pyhäinpäivä the first Saturday of November, and Janet's kids are usually there. You could come and meet with him yourself."

Bo hadn't been to the traditional Finnish gathering in years. "That sounds doable. I'd still like his information, if you get it sooner."

"Okay, but please come. Now that you're living in the Upper, there's no reason not to reconnect with your people here."

My people.

In the six months since he'd returned to Michigan, he'd visited his mother only a few times. She was a pillar in the Finnish community she'd grown up in. He'd grown up there, too, but only during his youngest years. His mother had recently retired from her administrative position at Finlandia University, but there was no relocating for her and never had been. Her roots ran so deep that she'd refused to marry his father because it would have meant moving away.

Bo's Finnish roots had been cut when he went to live with his father as a teen, after his grandfather died. Bo had been away from the local customs for so long, they didn't mean much more to him than fond memories of his youth. This was his heritage, and maybe it was time to embrace it once again.

"There's a candlelight walk through the woods this year, you know, if you care to bring someone."

He couldn't help but smile. His mother still had hopes that one day, he'd marry. Funny thing was that he had, but he couldn't breathe a word of it.

"We'll see," he finally said.

Maybe he'd ask Ruth to go with him so they could both talk to Janet's son. Knowing someone might give them an edge in getting a bid submitted.

"How are you really, son?"

"I'm buying into the tree business I've been working for. There's potential for growth but a lot to organize. It looks like I'm staying in the area." That much he could tell her.

"I knew you'd come home one day. I'm glad, Boothe. I truly am."

"Me too." That was also true. Since moving back to the Upper Peninsula and working with Cole, he finally felt like he fit. "I'll see you in a couple of weeks."

"And I'll text you the name of Janet's son and his info when I have it."

"Thanks, Mom." After disconnecting, he slipped into his jacket and headed out the door.

He'd grab lunch and put a deposit down on storing his Airstream for the winter. If an apartment didn't present itself, he'd have to consider taking Ruth's offer.

His hesitation to live in her garage apartment seemed to have offended her, as if he thought such an arrangement beneath him. It wasn't that at all. It was her. He found her attractive. Spending time with her in the office promised to be bad enough, but seeing her at home was bound to cause complications to their agreement. At least on his end.

He turned to prayer. *Lord, give me wisdom in this whole thing. Please.*

The passage of scripture in the book of James that he'd read this morning stated that God liberally gave wisdom to those who asked. Bo definitely needed some. Too much depended on him making not only good decisions but also wise ones.

Ruth's boys came to mind. They'd need wise treatment as well. Living on-site, he'd have an opportunity to reach out to Ethan and Owen. They deserved better than growing up without their father, and if Bo could help them somehow, it'd certainly ease his conscience.

Bo punched in the number to the last apartment contact on his list. There hadn't been many in Pine, and most were year-long leases, but he'd try. Getting voice mail, Bo left his name and number and reason for the call. He'd find out soon enough, but the apartment above Ruth's garage was looking more and more like the better option. Maybe even the wisest one.

Finally, the end of the week.

Ruth slumped in her dentist's waiting room Friday afternoon. After nearly two days of organizing Cole's office, she looked forward to a weekend off. But then again, she didn't. Weekends were lonely times.

When Cole was alive, the crew at Miller Logging and Tree Service often worked Saturdays to catch up. But since his death, new jobs barely trickled in. At this point, most of the work was repeat firewood business and tree removals. She hoped the crew was glad for a full weekend off even if it meant less pay.

Her cell phone rang.

"Hello?"

"Ruth, this is Bo."

A tremor passed through her at the sound of his voice. "Something wrong?"

A soft chuckle. "No. I received the revised contracts in the mail today. Would you like me to swing by and drop them off?"

"No." She wouldn't be home for an hour or so, and she didn't want those papers falling into or out of anyone's hands but hers.

Ruth couldn't expect Bo to hang around and wait for her either. He must still be in town, because he used a PO box for his mail. She'd checked the payroll records, and no physical address had been listed in Cole's paperwork for Boothe Harris.

"I'm at the dentist's office—"

"Sorry. I'll let you go. We can go over them Monday."

At the office. She wanted to review them sooner rather than later, and she wouldn't mind checking out this "camper" he lived in. "Or I could come to your place and sign them after I'm done here." Ruth cringed at how forward that sounded.

He didn't answer right away.

Yup, she'd put him on the spot. She looked up, as the dental hygienist had just come out for her. "Bo?"

"Yeah, that'd work. I'll text you the directions. Why don't you bring the boys as well?"

"Great. They'd love a change of scenery." She

would, too, but she wasn't going to admit that out loud.

"It's a nice night for a campfire."

Ruth smiled. He was right about that. The forecast promised a chilly but clear night. "I'll bring hot dogs."

He let out a breath as if he'd been holding it. "Sounds good. See you soon."

She disconnected.

"Big plans?" Gina had been a dental assistant when Ruth had worked here as the hygienist.

"No. Just a campfire with the boys." Ruth followed Gina into the office used for dental cleanings and slipped up onto the chair.

Gina squeezed her shoulder. "How are you?"

Ruth shrugged. "Hanging in there."

"Have you thought about coming back to work here? Dr. Gregg is expanding his practice."

"I let my license expire."

"He'll know what steps you need to take to recertify."

Ruth already knew those steps, and they'd be tough ones, considering she'd been out of this line of work for eight years. "Something to consider, I suppose."

"Especially if Miller Logging and Tree Service goes under."

Ruth sat up straighter. "Where'd you hear that?"

"Around. With Cole gone…" Again, Gina

squeezed her shoulder. "I just wish you the best, you know? And, well, times are tough."

Ruth leaned back and opened her mouth for Gina to start the cleaning process, but she didn't relax. So, word around town was Cole's business was headed south. She really should stop calling it Cole's. It was hers now, and it wasn't going down. Not if she could help it. Not with Bo Harris and his MBA from the Ross School of Business. They had to turn it around, and why couldn't they?

Logging was big business in the Upper Peninsula. It's just that Miller Logging and Tree Service had always been a smaller operation than most—but bigger than some. They didn't do the large logging jobs that supplied the major paper-product companies, but they did supply a couple of local mills. A lot of the wood they harvested ended up as firewood as well. Including the pile she had, still waiting to be stacked.

Ruth closed her eyes, but that didn't help her relax. She'd put all her eggs in the Boothe Harris basket, and if he didn't come through, then what? What if after marrying him to save the business, it still went under?

She had to give him a chance to prove himself. In the meantime, she'd learn everything she could from him. Starting tonight, with a campfire on his property.

Chapter Six

"Are we there yet?" Owen whined from the back seat.

"Not yet." Ruth glanced at her minivan's GPS. The turn should be any moment.

There.

She turned onto Spring Lake Road and checked her mileage. Bo's text had said that his place was three miles on the right. The road wasn't paved, but at least it had been graded. Dust billowed behind her, promising that her minivan would be filthy by the end of the night. No wonder Bo's black pickup was so dusty.

Ruth hoped she didn't get turned around heading back to Pine later. She'd told her mother-in-law not to expect them home until well after dark. Nora had simply smiled, looking immensely pleased, as if this were a date.

Ruth had corrected her real quick by explaining that tonight's meeting was about the business and reviewing the final buy-in agreement. But Nora hadn't been swayed, adding that it was nice of Bo to invite the boys.

Ruth had the distinct feeling that Bo wanted the boys along as a buffer. Not that she minded. Her boys would make the perfect chaperones, keeping her too busy for any personal conversation. And that might be both good and bad. She just wished Nora would stop seeing Bo as their modern-day Boaz.

Bringing her focus back to driving, Ruth noticed that there were few year-round homes on this road. She saw mostly two-track driveways with gates that were closed. She wondered if this might be a seasonal road. If so, the county might not snowplow all the way out here. There's no way Bo should stay out here through the winter months. Offering him the garage apartment made perfect sense.

At the three-mile mark of her odometer, Ruth took a right turn onto a wide crushed-gravel driveway. This had to be it, as there didn't appear to be any other driveways nearby. She peeked at her boys in the back seat. Both were gazing wide-eyed out their windows as they drove through a tunnel of trees in full autumn glory. Yellows and reds and peachy-orange leaves fluttered to the ground as they drove deeper into the canopy, deeper into the woods.

When they finally came to a vast clearing of

mowed grass, Ruth pulled off where the gravel driveway stopped. She spotted Bo's dust-covered pickup truck parked near a shiny silver travel trailer that screamed top-of-the-line expensive. The camper had been placed to capture perfect views of a small lake. An awning covered a flat wooden platform complete with a couple of camp-style rocking chairs. A firepit lay just beyond and it was already stacked with wood, ready to light.

"Wow," Ethan whispered. "This is nice."

"You're not kidding," Ruth agreed. She cut the engine, and the boys were already clicking out of their child seats and opening their doors. "Wait!"

Too late. They were running toward the iconic silver tube of an Airstream travel trailer.

Bo exited the camper. "Evening."

"Is this yours?" Ethan asked. "Can we go inside?"

"It is." Bo glanced at her. "You can, as long as it's okay with your mom."

Ethan and Owen both looked at her as well. All three of them waited for her answer.

"I will go in with you, and don't touch anything." Ruth stepped up onto the wooden platform and tapped it with her toe. "This is a good idea."

"Keeps the sand down." Bo opened the door for them.

The boys slipped in under his arm, so Ruth hurried inside to keep her eyes on them. The interior was far more impressive and expensive-looking than she'd expected. Tan leather seating with soft-looking throw pillows, big windows, a nice little kitchen and a separate bedroom. The colors were clean and neutral. Bo kept the place tidy.

"How long have you lived in this?" Ruth kept watch on her boys.

"Five years." Bo stood by the door, giving them space to look around.

Ethan stared with wide eyes while Owen ran his pudgy five-year-old hands over everything. Touching the couch, the tabletop—exactly what she'd told him not to do. Then off they went into Bo's bedroom.

"Stop!" She used her mom voice. "Do not go into that room without asking."

The boys halted and turned to Bo. "Can we look?"

Bo chuckled. "Sure. If you take your shoes off, you can even jump on the bed."

Ethan and Owen wasted no time in kicking off their shoes before launching themselves onto a neatly made bed.

"You're playing with fire there," Ruth muttered. She walked toward the bedroom to make sure the boys did nothing more than "jump on the bed."

"They can't hurt anything." Bo sounded from directly behind her. "It's sturdy."

And big. The bed had to be at least queen-size. There was what she assumed was a closet, but it was small. As was the chest of drawers. He must not have a lot of stuff, but what he had was quality. The colorful braided area rug by the bed was well made. A pair of expensive work boots had been kicked off in the corner, and an alarm clock sat atop a stack of books under a small lamp. Other than that, everything else must be tucked away.

She zeroed in on those books again. One of them was labeled *Holy Bible*, with a worn leather binding. Did he really read God's word, or had it been placed there, knowing she was coming here?

Whoa—why'd she continually question his motives? Because he seemed too good to be real, that's why.

Feeling the warmth of Bo standing behind her, Ruth stepped forward to examine a blanket draped at the foot of the bed. Running her fingers over the fine wool in hues of gray and slate blue, she glanced at Bo. She couldn't imagine a man buying it. "This is beautiful. Was it a gift?"

"In a way. I bought it for my grandmother when I was in Finland. My mom thought I should have it after she died."

"Oh." Sweet and sad, this work of woolen art.

Bo had been everywhere—from Finland to Alaska—while she'd been out of the state of Michigan only once, for her honeymoon to the Wisconsin Dells.

Ruth grabbed her sons' arms to still their jumping. "Okay, that's enough. Let's go outside."

With peals of laughter, the boys bounced down, picked up their sneakers and ran under Bo's arm toward the exit. She heard the soft click of the camper door. No screen door–sounding slams in this travel trailer.

Bo chuckled at her boisterous sons, but he hadn't moved from blocking the doorway.

Ruth caught him studying her and flushed. Then she pointed at the stack of books. "Do you read that Bible?"

"Yes." His expression was bland. Controlled.

Ruth narrowed her gaze, feeling the need to test him. "And what do you think?"

His mouth slipped into a crooked smile. "You want me to quote something as proof?"

Ruth chuckled. "It wouldn't hurt."

"Okay, the second chapter of James is all about treating others according to faith. Helping when someone is in need because faith without good deeds is dead."

Ruth chewed on that a bit. Maybe that's what she was—his good deed. "Okay, okay. Test passed. I better get outside and make sure they aren't in that lake."

Bo backed away, giving her room to pass. "Can I get you something to drink?"

"I brought pop and water." She spotted a single service coffee maker on the counter. "But I'd love a cup of coffee."

He smiled. "Tend your boys. I'll bring it out."

Ruth exited the sleek camper. It was a cool evening, and the northern nip in the air forewarned falling temperatures were not far off. Scanning the sandy shoreline of the lake, she saw that Ethan and Owen were messing with something close to the water's edge. "Please stay out of the water."

"It's a turtle," Ethan said.

"Leave it alone. It might be a snapper." Ruth sat in a rocking chair with a good view of her boys.

After they shooed the turtle back into the water, they moved on to throwing rocks. Ruth hoped that little turtle had gotten out of the way in time. She breathed in the sights as the sun hung low in the sky. She actually looked forward to watching it set, feeling more relaxed than she had in a long time.

"Here." Bo handed her a mug of steaming coffee with cream that smelled amazing.

"Thank you." Ruth took a sip and closed her eyes at the taste of strong liquid bliss.

Bo sat in the rocker next to her. "They seem to be enjoying themselves."

"Why wouldn't they? This place is amazing. How much land do you own here?"

"Fifty acres."

"Nice chunk. Did you just buy it?" She watched Owen pick up a large rock only to drop it, sending a splash of water all over the legs of his jeans. Ethan gathered sticks and placed them in the fire ring.

"I've had it for over five years."

"Any plans to build?" Ruth couldn't believe he'd been sitting on this acreage for so long without doing something with it.

"Eventually."

It was beautiful land, with a huge clearing that melted into hardwoods dotted with pine. It might be too pretty for a business, but it was the kind of land Cole would have wanted. If they could have ever afforded it.

Ruth looked at Bo, wondering just how much was in his trust fund. Nope, not going to ask. Ever. It was none of her business.

"Why travel when you had this to come home to?" Ruth hadn't meant it as a need-to-know question—more of an observation. That being said, she truly wanted to know what had prompted him to travel all the way to Alaska, where he'd spent the last three years of his gilded life as a woodcutter.

"I have the final contracts inside, if you'd like to look them over before signing."

"Sure." The coffee took on a bitter taste as the reality of why she'd come settled in along with his obvious dodge of her question.

Like she'd told Nora, this was business, not a date. Not a getting-to-know-you session. And she wasn't a girlfriend with the right to go digging around in his past *whys* and *why nots*. She wasn't looking for a relationship, but she could use a friend. Was that even possible with Bo, when he shared so little about himself?

While Ruth went over the final contracts inside the camper, Bo struck a long match and held it beneath the wood, watching as the single flame licked the small twigs until they caught. He focused on the spread of fire that seemed to mirror his feelings for Ruth. He hadn't planned on this growing attraction for her. He hadn't considered how dishonest he'd feel when he'd promised their marriage would be strictly for the business.

He noticed that her boys watched his every move. Ethan had added some sticks to the pile, which made Owen demand that his sticks be added too. He chuckled at how the boys competed. They argued, too, but there was genuine affection between them. No doubt the loss of their dad had cemented their brotherly bond.

He'd often wondered what his life would have been like had his mother married his father and he'd had a sibling or two. He only knew that his mother wouldn't leave her folks or her community, and his father wouldn't move north.

In spite of their decision to part ways, his parents had remained friendly. His mother had been granted full custody of him, but Bo had still visited his father on various odd holidays.

It wasn't until after his grandfather had died that Bo went to live with his father during the school year while he attended a private high school there.

"Give it back," Ethan hollered.

The kid's angry voice pierced Bo's thoughts and refocused his attention. "What's the problem?"

"I don't have it." Owen's dark gray eyes glittered with mischief.

If ever Bo had seen trouble as an expression, it was now, written all over the five-year-old's face. Bo stood and asked the elder boy again. "What's this about?"

Ethan barely looked at him as he yelled, *"Mom!"*

Ruth exited the camper, frustration clearly etched across her pretty face. "What is it, Ethan?"

"Owen took my fidget spinner. Again!"

"Did not."

Bo looked at Owen. The tyke kicked at the grass and wouldn't look at him.

"Give it back to your brother," Ruth scolded.

"I don't have it."

"Yes, he does. I left it on my chair, and now it's gone," Ethan explained.

Ruth looked under the camp chair. "Are you sure you didn't leave it in the car?"

Bo continued to gaze at Owen. The kid had taken it and wasn't fessing up.

"Owen," Ruth sighed. "Do you have it?"

The five-year-old shook his head.

"Yes, he does." Ethan stepped closer and pushed his brother hard enough to knock him down.

"Ethan!"

And then the tears started.

With the sound of Ruth's scolding, Owen's cries and Ethan's protests ringing in his ears, Bo reached for the bucket he used to douse campfires. Without a word, he ambled down to the water's edge, filled the bucket and returned.

The boys had quieted, and even Ruth watched him.

He gave Ruth a wink as he raised the bucket over the fledgling fire.

"What are you doing?" Ethan asked.

"It appears that you do not want a campfire."

Owen wiped at his tears. "Yeah, we do."

Bo knelt down to look the five-year-old in the

eye. "Then perhaps you should return what you took from your brother."

Sheepishly, Owen fished in his jeans pocket for the spinner and handed it over to Ethan.

Ruth's eyes widened, and then she mouthed the words *thank you*. To her youngest son, she crooked her finger. "Owen, come with me a moment."

The five-year-old did not look happy to follow his mom into the camper.

Bo chuckled, wondering if Ruth was going to give the tyke a hearty talking-to.

He turned to Ethan. "I think this fire could use a few more sticks before we toss the large logs on. Would you like to help me?"

Ethan shrugged but followed him to the edge of the woods.

They both gathered up a few more branches on the ground. Bo brought his back to the fire ring and dumped his stack on the side. Ruth had returned with a red-faced little boy wiping away his tears.

"Owen, I think your brother could use your help. He's got a lot of sticks to carry," Bo said.

The little guy didn't hesitate to run off and join Ethan.

"Sorry about that," Ruth whispered. "Owen has a habit of taking Ethan's stuff."

Bo cocked his head. "Why's that, do you think?"

"I don't know. Boys being boys, or maybe it's an attention thing." Ruth's brow furrowed. "What I won't tolerate is either of the boys lying. Owen lied about taking that spinner."

Bo saw the fury in Ruth's eyes and knew she wasn't kidding. Honesty was important to her. Crucial. Another kick in the gut. Not only had he not told her about the day Cole died, but he was also breaking their deal of keeping things strictly business by the growing attraction he had for her.

"Other than shattering the peace and quiet, no harm done." Bo added a few broken branches to the fire. Was it simply being brothers, or was there something Owen needed that made him target Ethan? Bo didn't know much about kids, but he'd keep his ears open on this one.

Owen raced back with a handful of sticks. "Will these do, Mr. Harris?"

Bo smiled as he took the offering and made a show of adding them to the low flames. "Nicely. See, they're already catching."

Ethan joined them with an armful that he dropped into a pile in the sandy ring around the firepit.

Bo looked to Ruth for permission. "Can Ethan help me add these to the fire?"

"Can I?" Ethan bounced a couple of times.

Ruth didn't look like she wanted him to, but

she gave her go-ahead. "Listen to what Mr. Harris tells you."

Ethan nodded.

Bo crouched by the fire ring. "Fire deserves respect. It's not something to play with. Add a couple sticks right there in that hole, and then step back."

"I know." Ethan did as asked but added quietly, "I've done this before with my dad."

"Of course." Bo couldn't look the kid in the eye.

That simple reminder without a hint of Ethan's usual sarcasm ripped open the wound all over again. Bo concentrated on the fire, but the memory of Cole's lifeless body took front and center in his mind. He was a fool to think he could fill the void of Cole's death, but part of him wanted to try.

Flames licked the larger sticks Ethan had provided with a snap and crackle. The boys darted off once again to hunt for more dry sticks in the small woods on the other side of the driveway.

"Have you thought any more about taking the apartment over the garage?" Ruth's deep voice was whisper soft.

"I have." Tonight, seeing those boys had cinched it. "I will take it and pay you the going rate."

Ruth laughed. "I don't think there's a going rate for studio apartments in Pine."

"We'll figure it out."

"I suppose we will." Ruth looked at him. "You can move in anytime, even this weekend."

Bo nodded. There was no reason to delay. He'd already paid for the covered storage, and his spot waited for him to park the Airstream. "Sounds good."

"And thanks for having us out here. The boys needed this." Ruth looked at him, her smile sweet. "You're pretty good with them."

He wasn't prepared for the rush of warmth that washed over him at the compliment. He might not know much about kids, but he knew what it had been like to be a kid without the daily influence of his father. Like Owen, Bo had sought attention and approval in various ways after his grandfather had died. Some good, some bad.

Bo hoped he could have a good influence on Ruth's boys. Making a positive impact on anyone took time, and that's something he'd have more of living above their garage.

The next morning, Ruth wasn't surprised to get a text from Bo asking if he could swing by and drop off a few of his things.

She replied that he was welcome anytime, she'd leave the door to the apartment open and he'd find the stairs on the back side of the garage.

Nora entered the kitchen. "What has you smiling?"

Ruth looked up from her phone. Had she been smiling? She definitely enjoyed this quiet moment at the breakfast nook while the boys watched a movie in the family room, so that must be it. Besides, it was relaxing to linger over the last of the coffee while rain drizzled outside.

"Ruth?" Nora tipped her head. "You okay?"

"Yep, just fine." Ruth considered how to best broach the subject of their new tenant, gave up and went with blunt. "I offered Bo the apartment above the garage for the winter."

"Oh?" Nora looked as if she tried to contain her pleasure and failed.

Ruth couldn't exactly share in the excitement, even if she had been smiling when she'd read Bo's text. Sure, she was glad he'd given in and taken the apartment as if it were an I-told-you-so moment, but was she ready to see him daily outside of their workplace?

Nora filled the teakettle and set it on the stove. "When is he moving in?"

"Looks like this weekend. He just texted me that he'd drop off some of his things today."

Nora's eyes widened. "We need to get up there and clean it."

"It's fine. I took care of that after Cash left." She'd stripped the bed and had cleaned out the fridge after Cole's brother had returned to his unit with the Marines.

"That was over a month ago. There's probably

dust all over up there." Nora wasn't having any of it and promptly gathered cleaning supplies from under the sink.

Ruth wasn't going to let her do it alone, so she gave in. "Okay, okay, we'll clean it."

"Can't have a man like Bo Harris moving into a dirty apartment."

"Of course not." Ruth held back a laugh.

Nora simply smiled. "I'm glad he's moving in."

"Over the garage," Ruth clarified.

"I know that, but it will be nice having him here, looking out for us."

There was no use stating that Ruth had looked out for them just fine, because that wasn't quite true. It had taken Boothe Harris and his intervention to suspend foreclosure. Because of that, her mother-in-law had placed Bo on the hero pedestal as their *kinsman redeemer.*

Ruth sighed, gulped the last of her coffee and stood. "Okay, mother-in-law of mine, let's get this done while the boys are occupied."

Nora smiled. "I'll tell them where we're going."

Ruth grabbed the apartment key and vacuum cleaner, then slipped on her raincoat and headed outside into the cold, drizzly rain.

"Let me take that." Bo's voice came from out of nowhere.

Startled, Ruth looked up, causing the hood of

her raincoat to slip from her head. Rain dampened her cheeks, but it glistened in tiny droplets hanging on to the ends of Bo's shaggy hair. "Wow. That was fast. I just texted you."

He gave her a crooked half smile. "I texted you earlier, before I headed into the office."

"Oh." She hadn't paid any attention to the time of his text. Ruth handed over the vacuum and followed him up the stairs to the apartment. "What did you go in to do?"

"Took some measurements for another desk, and I wanted to review the books. I plan to call on the mills we supply and some of the larger customers from some years ago to see if they have any current needs." He stepped aside on the small landing, giving her room to open up the apartment.

Why hadn't she thought of that? Ruth stopped on the step below him, feeling dwarfed in more ways than his height. "Good idea."

Again with the half smile. "Yes."

She narrowed her gaze at the simple answer. Was that arrogance leaking from his eyes? He had an MBA; of course he'd know how to prospect new jobs. He didn't need her kudos. When it came to Miller Logging and Tree Service, he probably didn't need her at all.

Wait… She was his ticket to the trust fund. She shook off those snarky thoughts, stepped up, squeezed around him and opened the door. "Here it is."

He went inside, set the vacuum down and looked around. He appeared surprised by what he saw. "Nice."

"Yes." Copying his terse response, Ruth refrained from adding the *I told you so* that hung on her tongue.

His half smile turned lopsided. "Were you coming up to clean it?"

Ruth felt her cheeks heat. "My mother-in-law—"

"Bo, you're here." Nora stepped into the apartment with her basket of cleaning supplies. "We didn't expect you so soon."

"I can certainly take care of cleaning this place." He looked around again. "Not that it needs it."

Ruth had the absurd urge to tell Nora that she told her so as well.

"Nonsense." Nora waved him away. "We'll take care of it, and it won't take us long."

"Lunchtime isn't too far away. I'd like to bring back pizza for us with my next load. Is there one you prefer?"

Ruth considered his offer.

Nora jumped in and answered first. "Anything is fine, but the boys like plain cheese."

"Noted. I'll grab my stuff." Bo left, his footsteps barely audible on the wooden steps outside.

And Ruth turned toward her mother-in-law. "Pizza?"

Nora shrugged. "Why not? The boys will love it. Plus, you can tell them about Bo moving in."

Ruth's stomach flipped, reacting to those two little words—*moving in?* "Over the garage, and he's only here for the winter."

"Of course." Nora smiled.

Ruth didn't quite understand her mother-in-law's full-court press when it came to Bo. Plugging in the vacuum, Ruth had a bad feeling that this was going to be a very long winter.

Chapter Seven

Four days later, Ruth rushed into the Pine Wood Inn's café. She was running late after having a longer-than-necessary phone conversation with a potential customer she couldn't hand over to Bo. He'd been out with Frank, giving a quote on clear cutting. She'd texted Bo about it before she'd left, though, letting him know she wouldn't be back to the office this afternoon.

There was no way she'd miss lunch with Maddie and Erica. It had been almost two weeks since their last meeting because of her dentist appointment, and Ruth had a lot to share. A whole lot. She spotted the other two widows in their usual window seat and waved.

Erica waved back.

"Sorry I'm late." Ruth slipped into a seat.

"No worries. We haven't ordered yet." Erica looked as if she'd just come in from a hike with her dark hair pulled back and a slight sheen of sweat still visible along her hairline.

Ruth turned to Maddie. "How are you both?"

Maddie shrugged. "Nothing to report other than the house next door finally sold. I'm hoping for nice neighbors."

Ruth shared a look with Erica. They were both worried about Maddie withdrawing into herself. The last few meetings, she'd shared so little. Of course, Ruth had too much to share, but still.

She touched Maddie's arm. "Want to talk about it?"

"Nope." Maddie shook her head. "Nothing to talk about. What about you? Are you going to marry that guy?"

Ruth scrunched her nose. "I already did. Please keep it quiet, though. No one knows, not even Nora."

Both women made their solemn sign of two fingers against their lips in salute. And then they laughed. Their lunch dates were more than for grieving together—they'd become their own club. A widows' club.

"So how is this business marriage?" Erica asked.

Ruth took a deep breath and let it out. "Well, foreclosure has been averted, we have a couple new customers with decent projects on the horizon and this past weekend, Bo moved into the apartment over the garage."

"Wow, so he's living close. Why?" Erica wasn't one to beat around the bush.

Ruth wondered if Erica's direct nature resulted from being an RN. Whatever it was, Erica had a talent for weeding through the peripheral information and getting right to the sore spot.

With Bo living so close, she saw more of him, and so did her boys. The day he'd moved in, he'd bought them pizza, which they'd eaten together in her cozy kitchen. It felt far too family-like for her comfort. Her boys must have felt it too. Owen had asked Bo to stay and play games with him, but Ethan had grown quiet and watchful. Every word she and Bo had exchanged seemed to be visually dissected by her eight-year-old.

Fortunately, Bo had declined staying. He had plenty of believable excuses—finish moving his things as well as prep his travel trailer for storage. But Ruth didn't buy either of those as the real reasons for his quick escape after lunch. He'd run like a scared jackrabbit, and that had made Ruth laugh. Maybe the cozy family atmosphere was a little too much for Bo as well.

Ruth took a sip of the water that had been placed there before she'd arrived. "He's been living in a camper and needed to store it for the winter. He couldn't find a month-to-month apartment."

"So you offered your place?" Erica prodded.

Ruth glanced at Maddie, who smiled in agreement with Erica. They both wanted to know the real reason Ruth had invited Bo to move in, so to speak. She paused a moment to glance at the menu as their waitress bore down on their table for their orders. No problem, as Ruth ordered the same elaborate salad plate every time.

Once the waitress left, Ruth faced her friends. "I wanted to keep my eye on him, you know? Make sure he's for real."

"What makes you think he's not?" Erica asked.

"Yeah." Maddie nodded.

Ruth thought about that. So far this week, Bo had mowed her lawn and offered to paint her recently installed picket fence as payment for rent when she wouldn't give him a price. He'd even asked if Ethan wanted to help, and her oldest, surprisingly, had agreed.

Ruth shrugged. "I don't know. It's like this whole arrangement is too good to be true but horrible as well. Cole hired him, and he wouldn't do that if there was something wrong with the guy, something bad—but still. Bo's actually a distant cousin, and although I called *him*, I feel like he's orchestrated this whole deal and I don't know why."

"Maybe he wants access to his trust fund," Maddie offered.

Ruth considered that regularly. "I don't know. He's lived in an Airstream travel trailer for the past five years and seems perfectly content with it. He doesn't have a lot of stuff."

"That you know of," Erica added.

"True, but everything I've seen so far points to his leading a simple life."

"Until now," Maddie added.

"Yes, that's right. Now it's—I don't know." Ruth shrugged.

"You've gotten to know him pretty well," Erica said.

"I don't know him at all. That's why I offered him the apartment. I need to figure out why he'd change his life this way—" Her voice broke. "For me."

"Maybe he's just a good guy who wants to help." Maddie's voice held a note of wistful longing.

"Attractive?" Erica added.

Ruth laughed. "Uh, yeah, very."

"Hmm." Erica sat back as their lunches arrived.

The three of them bowed their heads as Erica prayed over the food, but Ruth couldn't concentrate. She kept seeing the solemn look in Bo's icy eyes when he'd suggested that they marry. He hadn't been flippant about it, nor had the idea seemed like a new toy for a rich trust fund guy to try. He'd been thoughtful and earnest, as if he owed it to her—

Ruth felt the touch of Maddie's hand and looked up. "What?"

"We're done praying."

"Oh." Ruth felt her cheeks blaze.

"Are you attracted to this man?" Erica's keen gaze didn't miss a thing. "Because it's okay if you are."

"No, it's not. Cole's only been gone—" Ruth felt her throat closing up with emotion.

Both Maddie and Erica gripped her hands.

She squeezed in return. "I miss Cole. I miss what we had, and..."

Ruth couldn't go on; her throat was too tight. Of the three of them, Ruth had been the only one with a truly happy marriage. She'd been the most recently widowed, too, and yet she was the one talking about another man in her life.

"It's okay, Ruth. God sends people we need when we need them. Don't beat yourself up for being human." Again, Erica's wisdom rang true.

Ruth missed her husband. It might be natural for her to want to lean on Bo because she'd depended on Cole for so many things. Still, she didn't have to surrender to nature, nor her desire to be taken care of.

If what Erica said was indeed true, Ruth needed to thank God for sending Bo to save Cole's business and their home and leave it at that. She needed to accept this arrangement as a business deal and quit trying to read more into it than was there.

From now on, she'd concentrate on only what she could control—her emotions and reactions to this attractive man who'd turned her financial situation around.

Saturday morning, Bo grabbed the bucket of paint he'd purchased at the hardware store along with brushes and containers. He'd tackle Ruth's picket fence since the weather was dry and relatively mild. He tucked a couple of clean rags into his back pocket.

Checking his watch, he didn't think eight thirty was too early to see if Ethan wanted to join him. He quickly texted Ruth to let her know what he was up to. It wasn't long before he received a reply.

Owen wants to help too. Is that okay?

He chuckled and texted back that it was fine.

By the time he made it down the stairs from his apartment, both boys were waiting for him in the backyard. And Ruth.

"Morning," he said.

"Good morning." Her smile was bright. "I'm headed to the grocery store. Is there anything you need?"

"Nope, I'm good."

"Nora's here. If the boys act up, just send them to her."

"Noted." Bo looked at both Miller boys. "I think we'll be okay."

Owen smiled, and Ethan might have rolled his eyes, but Bo couldn't be sure. He wondered if Ruth had made the older boy come out and help, because the kid didn't look too keen on the task ahead.

Bo set down the supplies and rubbed his hands together. "All right, let's get started on this side."

It was the shortest length of fence that ran from the house to the garage. Bo opened the bucket, stirred and then divided the white paint into three plastic bowls, which he handed to each boy along with a brush.

"We can spread out a little." Bo figured they'd meet up in the middle.

Ethan took the end near the garage. Owen knelt near his brother, so Bo started near the house. He hoped they could get one side done before he headed for his property to disconnect the travel trailer and park it in storage.

He dipped his brush in paint, then spread it on the fence. The thirsty wood soaked it in. A second coat would definitely be needed. With quick, even strokes, Bo covered one slat, then two, making sure to get the sides covered as well. After fifteen minutes or so, he checked on the boys.

Owen had more paint on his hands than on the fence. Ethan was much further along.

"Try to get the sides too," Bo pointed out.

Ethan nodded. "I was going to do that on the way back."

"Good plan." Bo returned to his end.

After another fifteen minutes or so, Owen was at his side, watching him. "What's up?"

Owen had paint on the end of his nose. "Nothing."

Bo kept painting, but the task proved more tedious than he'd anticipated. Taking longer too. He glanced at Ethan, and the boy looked like he was already weary of it.

"Why are we painting?" Owen asked.

"To protect the wood against the weather, and it will look nicer," Bo explained.

"I don't want to paint no more," Owen said.

"That's fine." Bo couldn't send the five-year-old to his grandmother with paint all over the kid's hands. "Maybe we should wash up a little before you go inside."

Bo set his brush down and scanned the back of the house for a garden hose. Once spotted, he walked over to Ethan. "How are you doing?"

Ethan shrugged.

The kid was actually doing a pretty good job.

"I'd like to rent a paint sprayer for the rest of

the fence. It'll be faster for sure. What do you think?"

Ethan looked up at him then. "Good idea."

"Your brother is done. I'm going to help him wash his hands. You can quit anytime you want."

Ethan considered it as he looked over the length of fence yet to finish. "I can paint a little more."

Bo smiled at the kid's grit. "Me too. After I take care of Owen."

Ethan nodded.

"Come on, Owen, let's rinse you off." Startled when the little guy slipped a paint-covered hand into his, Bo glanced down.

Owen looked up and grinned.

Bo smiled back and gave the pudgy little hand a squeeze. He was a cute kid who made Bo feel ten feet tall. He rinsed Owen's hands the best he could, considering the water turned cold quick. He handed him a rag. "Dry them good."

"Okay." Owen did his best.

Bo turned when he heard the side door open.

"How's it going?" Nora asked.

"Owen's done, and his hands will need a good washing. Ethan and I will finish this side, but I'm going to rent a sprayer for the rest of it."

"Thank you for doing this—and for everything, really."

Uncomfortable with the gratitude shining from her eyes, Bo held up a hand. "I appreciate having a place to stay through the winter. It's the least I can do."

Nora smiled as she ushered Owen into the house.

Bo turned back toward Ethan. If an eight-year-old wasn't ready to give up yet, then neither was he.

Late the next afternoon, Bo set his plate in the sink and stared at it. One dish from the meal he'd purchased at the corner grocery store on his way back from storing his Airstream. A meal for one. He'd been alone for a lot of years, but today it bit hard. Maybe it was knowing that Ruth and Nora and the boys were all tucked around a wooden table in their kitchen that had him so melancholy.

In the week since he'd moved in, Bo returned from work later than Ruth, after dark. Most nights, he'd climbed the stairs leading to this apartment without a peep from anyone in the house. Other than yesterday's painting of the fence, he'd seen little of Ruth's boys.

Ethan had hung in with him to finish one coat on the shortest length of fence. Ruth had been thrilled when she saw it. Bo had spotted pride in Ethan's eyes, and that was when he realized that her oldest son wasn't out there to help him, but his mom. Or maybe, more to the point, Ethan didn't want Bo to get all the credit. Regardless of the motivation, he had to admire the kid's work ethic. Ethan was no slacker.

Disconnecting the well and septic hookups had taken longer than expected, so he hadn't been able to move the travel trailer until today. He'd returned to eat dinner and watch football, but neither had satisfied. He scanned the spacious one-room apartment complete with a kitchenette and seating area that included a flat-screen TV and even a small woodstove. It was cozy and comfortable but felt empty.

More like the emptiness was in him.

Restless, Bo stretched, anxious to get back outdoors. He clicked Record on the TV for the rest of the football game, threw on a Sherpa-lined flannel along with a pair of work gloves and headed out.

Curving around the back side of the garage, he took in the large pile of carefully split firewood. Each log had been cut small on purpose. He grabbed a log and started a new row next to the pitiful stack of what must have been last year's wood.

One log turned into two, then five, then ten.

Bo heard the sound of rapid footsteps coming toward him and glanced up.

"Whatcha doing?" Owen watched him, his dark gray eyes serious.

"Stacking firewood. Want to help?" Bo didn't break his rhythm.

The five-year-old nodded but didn't move. He didn't seem to know what to do.

"We need to stack the wood like so. Don't shove the short ones in too deep. Keep the ends as even as you can." Bo handed the little guy a smaller log.

Owen placed the log and gently tapped the end to line it up with the other logs.

Bo smiled. "Good job."

Owen grabbed another small log. "Why do you live in Uncle Cash's house?"

Bo chuckled. "I couldn't find an apartment in town. Your mom said Uncle Cash won't be back for a while."

"He's a soldier." The kid's chin went up a notch. Owen was proud of his uncle.

"I know."

"Were you ever a soldier?" Owen dropped the log he was carrying and stooped to pick it up.

"Nope."

"How come?"

Bo laughed at the question but then thought for a moment.

"I chose a different path, I guess."

"Like in the woods?"

Bo nodded. "Yes, just like in the woods when there's more than one way to go."

The boy looked thoughtful. "Is it hard to cut down trees?"

"Sometimes." Bo marveled at the five-year-old's rapid-fire questions.

"My dad got killed by a tree," the boy said.

That statement cut Bo's heart in two. Dare he tell Owen that he'd been there? Maybe someday. "I know."

"What if a tree kills you too?" Owen asked.

Did the kid look at trees as monsters? Actually, some were, but not the way this boy viewed them. Bo knelt down so he could look him in the eyes. "Owen, what happened to your dad was an accident. One that doesn't happen often. It wasn't the fault of the tree or your dad. It just happened."

His stomach turned. The fault most likely lay with him. If only Bo could remember securing the pull rope correctly.

He heard heavier footfalls this time and looked up again.

"My dad used to do it different." Ethan pointed at the line of stacked wood.

Bo smiled. "I wish he were here to show me. Do you want to show me the best way?"

Ethan shrugged.

"Sounds like you know how," Bo coaxed.

Ethan didn't move, so Bo continued to stack the wood. Pretty soon, Ethan started handing him logs, and it helped speed things up somewhat.

Ruth appeared with a bottle of water and

small work gloves for the boys. "We can all help."

"Thanks." Bo took the water from her and downed it in one long gulp. The air was cool and crisp, but he'd grown hot with exertion. He handed the empty bottle back to Ruth.

She quickly looked away as she stashed the crushed plastic in the pocket of her hooded sweatshirt. "Here, boys, put these on."

"Like Mr. Harris?" Owen stuck out his hands.

"Yes, like Mr. Harris." Ruth helped her youngest with the gloves but handed the other pair to Ethan.

Ruth looked pretty, with her glorious red hair gathered into a long ponytail. She wore the same jeans with a heart-shaped patch on the knee that he'd noticed at work the other day. Same sturdy boots too.

"Have you had dinner?" she asked, grabbing a couple of logs from the pile.

"Yes." He continued to stack the wood Ethan handed him after fixing some of the awkward placements made by Owen's little hands.

"Boys, let's make a line and hand the wood to Mr. Harris." Ruth lined them up, then looked at him. "It goes faster this way."

"This is how my dad did it." Ethan's eyes held a challenge.

"Your dad was a smart man. Your mom is smart too." Bo gave her a wink.

"Okay, let's cut the chatter and get as much done as we can before it gets dark. You boys have school tomorrow, so it's a bath before bed."

The boys both groaned at the word *bath*. Some things never changed. He'd hated Sunday-night baths, too, at their age.

Ruth handed the logs Owen chose over to Ethan.

Ethan carried them to Bo.

It sped things up some, but Bo kept his eye on Ruth, who was clearly trying to hold it together. Obviously, this had been a family event with Cole. Bo could only imagine what memories might be going through her head right now.

The boys quieted, as if sensing the sorrow in their mom or dealing with their own memories. Until Owen piped up with yet another inquiry.

"Mr. Harris, are you going to marry my mom?"

"Owen, quit asking questions." Ruth glanced at Bo. He gave her an awkward smile that was barely a curve of his lips.

Ethan caught the look between them and threw down the log he was carrying. "I'm done."

"Ethan!" Ruth straightened, taking a step to go after her son.

Bo reached out to stop her, his voice soft. "Let him go."

Ruth shrugged off his touch. "I can't do that."

"Ethan?" She found him in the family room, slouching on the couch with the TV remote in his hand, staring at a blank screen. He looked ready to cry. "Ethan."

"Why's *he* got to be here?" His golden eyes shone with fury.

Ruth sat next to him, careful not to smother or crowd him into taking flight. "You saw his camper. He couldn't stay out there all winter."

Ethan looked at her, tears filling his eyes. "You like him."

Those three little words pierced her heart with searing shame. Hadn't she admitted as much to Erica and Maddie? But what had she done to give her eight-year-old son that idea?

Ruth swallowed hard, deciding to be as truthful as she could be without fessing up to the attraction she felt for Bo. "Of course I like him, Ethan. He's your dad's second cousin. Mr. Harris is helping me run the business, and I need his help."

Softer, she added, "Your dad would have wanted me to do whatever I could to keep the business going for you and Owen. He trusted Mr. Harris."

But should she?

A tear rolled down her son's cheek. "I wish Dad was here."

Tears gathered in her own eyes, but Ruth fought against letting them fall. "I miss him, too, sweetie. I will always love your father. Always."

Ethan sniffed and wiped his nose on the sleeve of his sweatshirt.

Ruth threaded her fingers through her boy's hair. Dare she share the depth of her heartache with her son? Could an eight-year-old even understand the lack of companionship that plagued her? The loneliness?

Cole had been killed nearly three months ago, and yet he was still part of who she was. Her dreams had been wrapped up into one man who'd been snatched away from her. When she'd kissed her husband goodbye that morning, she'd had no idea it'd be the last kiss. The last touch.

"Always means forever, no matter what. Now, I'm going back out there to help with the wood. Not because I want to, but because it's the right thing to do. Are you with me?"

Ethan looked at her with wide eyes and then, hanging his head, nodded.

Pride washed over her, causing those tears to gather all over again. Losing his dad had made Ethan grow up in some ways, but Ruth couldn't expect too much. He was only eight. She couldn't be a male role model for her boys. Not like Cole. She was their mom, and that's all she could be.

Opening her arms, she whispered, "I love you, Ethan."

He nodded again and leaned into her, wrapping his arms around her. "I love you, too, Mom."

She patted his back. "Let's go."

They walked outside, and Ruth nearly laughed hearing Owen badger Bo with more questions. Had he ever ridden a horse, what was his favorite color and did he like candy?

"I like chocolate candy," Bo answered, still stacking wood.

At their approach, he looked up and smiled with relief. "Thanks for coming back."

"You're welcome." Ruth handed Ethan a log.

Ethan handed it to Bo without looking him in the eye.

But Bo looked at Ethan, and he nodded toward Owen. "I was running out of answers."

Ethan looked up then and gave Bo a hint of a smile.

Ruth's heart full, she thanked the Lord for this small moment with a big victory. She kept handing over the logs, which had been split small because Frank knew it'd be her and the boys or Nora hauling them into the house for the fireplace. She appreciated that small gesture, as much as she appreciated Bo tackling the pile.

No matter how attracted to Boothe Harris she might be, Ruth couldn't let her flesh lead her into a place she wasn't yet ready to go. A place Ethan wasn't ready for her to go. For her sons' sake, Ruth needed to keep her wits and a respectful distance when it came to her handsome business partner.

Chapter Eight

The following morning, Bo woke up an hour before his alarm went off. He stared at the ceiling, replaying last night's wood stacking with Ruth and the boys that had ended with hot chocolate. Nora had brought out cups of the stuff made with milk and real cocoa. It had to be the best he'd ever tasted.

She'd invited him in as well, but he declined. After Ethan's reaction, Bo didn't want to push the kid. He didn't want to put Ruth on the spot either.

He got up, went to the bathroom and then padded to the kitchenette sink. He went about making a pot of dark roast with the auto-drip coffee maker he'd purchased. He had time to kill before he had to leave for work.

He hoped today went well with Ruth. He was no teacher, and trying to show her how to run a business was tough. He sounded too much like a boss rather than a partner, giving her instructions and orders. Sometimes she'd ask questions, but other times she'd narrow those golden eyes of hers as if weighing the truth of his words. She still didn't trust him. Not yet.

So far, they'd organized the office, utilizing the software Cole had purchased but never installed. Ruth had brought in both his phone and laptop to the office. Together, they'd transferred the billing process completely online with a 15 percent discount for customers who paid at the time of contract. Both he and Frank had the ability to accept credit card payments, in addition to cash or check, and generate an emailed receipt with a copy for Ruth's record keeping. So far, it had been working well.

Ruth's role had morphed into office manager. For now, she routed calls, continued with billing and payroll, and basically kept the office neat and tidy. He wasn't sure if that's what she really wanted. They needed to talk about that.

Today, they'd planned to update the company website, and he hoped it'd be something Ruth would take over. He wasn't good at that sort of thing, and truth be told, he didn't like being confined to the office. He wanted to be outside, working as much as possible.

The scent of brewing coffee filled the studio apartment. He waited for that last push of water through the filter before fixing himself a cup; then he padded toward one of the windows. There were only two in this space: one faced the back of the house and the other offered a view of the backyard. He glanced through the mini-blinds toward the house. All was dark there but for one dimly lit room.

He spotted Ruth working out on an elliptical machine through the slider. Dressed in leggings and a long T-shirt, with her hair pulled up into a ponytail that swayed with her movements, she bounced up and down, arms pushing the handles in rhythm with her feet. He admired the fast pace she kept, then stepped away after a couple more seconds, feeling like a creeper. She'd be mortified if she knew he'd watched her work out, even if only for a few seconds.

He wanted to earn her trust but knew it would take time. The same went for Ethan. Bo read such caution in their golden eyes. Ethan's coloring was similar to Ruth's, while Owen resembled Cole. The little one treated him like a shiny new toy. Hopefully, Bo wouldn't end up discarded when Owen tired of him.

After Bo had eaten, showered and read his daily portion of the Bible, he headed out the door and down the stairs. The temperature had dipped low last night, and thick frost lay on the ground and the windshield of his truck. He started the engine, then grabbed an ice scraper from the back seat.

"Morning." Ruth's voice captured his attention. She herded her two boys forward, into the garage bay.

"Morning." He nodded.

The boys' breath made little white puffs in the cold morning air. Ethan carried a backpack slung over one shoulder while Owen dragged his on the ground.

Owen held out his pudgy bare hand to reveal cereal. "Want some Cheerios?"

"No, but thank you. I had my breakfast." He couldn't keep the amusement out of his voice.

"Who made it?" The five-year-old looked puzzled.

"I did." Bo smiled. "Scrambled eggs."

Owen glanced at his mom. "I don't like eggs."

"Since when?" Ruth rolled her eyes. "Owen, get in the car."

Ethan had already climbed into the back seat. He slumped down and twirled something shiny between his fingers.

"See you at work." Bo finished scraping his windshield. The back window was nearly defrosted.

Ruth nodded as she buckled Owen into his seat. After climbing behind the wheel of her minivan, she tried starting the car, but the engine wouldn't turn over. She tried again: nothing.

He stepped into the garage to help. The second bay had Cole's truck parked inside with stuff packed in front of it. The lawnmower and plastic tubs were stacked against the tailgate. Obviously, Ruth hadn't used the truck in a while. And it'd take too long to get everything out of the way to back it out.

Ruth got out, looking frustrated.

"Sounds like your battery is dead. I can give you a lift."

She nodded. "We'll need Owen's car seat. Ethan's booster too. It's not that far to their school." Then, to her boys, she said, "Let's get into Mr. Harris's truck."

Backpack in hand, Ethan slipped out, as did Owen, but the little tyke was full of questions. "Do you know where my school is?"

"I'll show him, Owen. Now, get out of the car."

Bo bent forward to grab the car seat, but it was firmly attached. Looking for where it connected with the belt, he finally gave up and glanced at Ruth. "How do you unhook this thing?"

She leaned forward, her arm brushing his. "It's under here."

Once again, he noticed her soft scent. And how near she was. Before he could get out of her way, the car seat was free, and Ruth hauled it out, leaving behind a stream of cereal, pretzels and who knew what other kinds of crumbs from underneath that seat.

Bo hurried to open the back door of his truck. Ruth didn't look like she wanted to show him how to anchor the car seat, so he didn't offer. Instead, he fetched Owen's backpack, which had been left in the minivan. He also grabbed Ethan's booster seat. It came out much easier.

"Thanks. We're running a little late as it is."

"I'll drive fast." He gave Owen a wink as he handed him the pack, causing the kid to giggle.

She shot him a look as she took the booster and clicked it into place.

He raised his hands. "Kidding."

Ruth climbed into the passenger seat, turned and addressed her boys. "Do you have everything?"

"Yeah," both boys chorused.

Bo climbed in the now-warm truck. "Just tell me where to go."

It was mere minutes to the school. As Bo drove into line behind other parents dropping off kids, he mentioned the obvious. "Not too far of a walk."

"See, told you, Mom," Ethan piped up.

"When you're in middle school, and not before." Ruth gave Bo a hard look that clearly said when it came to her kids, his opinions were not wanted.

She slipped out of the passenger side when they came to a stop at the drop-off point, and he watched as she darted around to the other side to make sure Owen got out safely. Drawing both boys in for a quick hug, he heard her use that mom voice. "Grandma will pick you up after school. Ethan, don't forget to get your brother from class."

He couldn't hear what Ethan said, but the kid had nodded, his lips barely moving.

She quickly climbed back into the truck, but her gaze remained on the boys walking toward the school's entrance.

"Ready?"

Ruth nodded, but she didn't look away from her kids.

Hearing the horn beep behind him, Bo shifted into Drive and slowly rolled away from the school. Glancing at Ruth, he noticed that she was still staring out the window.

"Are you okay?" Surely he hadn't been that out of line with his walk-to-school comment.

She looked at him then. "You can drop me back at the house, and I'll get that truck started."

"Cole's truck?" That's what had her so forlorn.

She nodded and her eyes filled with tears.

"When was the last time you were in it?"

"Before Cole died. Frank's the one who drove it home after—" She cleared her throat. "After the accident."

Bo's gut clenched as images of that day assaulted him once again. Facing that truck would be more than tough, and he didn't want Ruth to do it alone. "Ride with me. We can stop and pick up a battery, and I'll change it when we get home."

Home.

The word rang uncomfortably loud in the silence that settled over them, but Ruth nodded in agreement.

After a few minutes, Ruth finally spoke. "I need to sell that truck."

He got the distinct feeling that there was a lot more meaning in those words than simply getting rid of a vehicle. "I can help."

"I might take you up on that." She gave him a slight smile and then turned in her seat. "Can I ask you something?"

His gut tightened. "Sure."

"Were you there when Cole died?"

Heat washed over him, and his head felt light. "I was."

"Frank said it was quick. Do you think Cole was in pain?" Ruth's eyes begged for reassurance.

At least he could give her that. "It was instant. He wasn't conscious."

He should tell her everything. Sweat broke out along his spine as he waited for her to ask another question. If she asked, he'd tell. But she didn't. And he realized he couldn't.

In that stretch of silence, something seemed

to shift between them. The wariness that often shone in her eyes had subsided. If this was an attempt to place her trust in him, he'd do everything in his power to prove that she'd made the right decision.

At the office, Ruth slipped into Cole's old chair and booted up the laptop computer while Bo made coffee. He'd refused to take over Cole's office, stating that he'd be out in the field more times than not.

So here she was, with a pretty shamrock plant on her desk and a picture frame sporting both boys' school pictures. She couldn't handle a family photo with her dead husband looking out at her—not since she'd married Bo. Even if it was a business deal, she couldn't shake the notion that she'd betrayed Cole.

Bo had been there when Cole died. He'd confirmed Frank's words that it had been instant. Frank had said that they'd tried CPR, but it hadn't worked. Cole was gone. And Bo had looked visibly shaken when asked about it. It was no wonder that he'd had empathy for her grief. He'd seen Cole die.

The aroma of the strong roast teased her senses. Cole had shared her love for bold coffee, but they'd enjoyed the good stuff at home. Plain old regular coffee had always been used at work. Until Bo had started bringing in his own gourmet blend for that first pot.

She glanced at him through the open window of Cole's office. It was a large slider that looked out over the rest of the trailer. "Smells good."

"It'll be done soon," Bo said. "I'll bring you a cup before the guys get at it."

"Thanks." She glanced out the other window in the office with a view of the yard.

Frank was walking toward the entrance as several trucks pulled in and parked. This time of year, before daylight saving time kicked in, the crew arrived just after sunrise in order to start work by eight thirty. They'd drain that coffeepot in no time.

The office trailer wasn't large; there were only three rooms. The main area housed a few chairs and a table in the corner, as well as a small fridge, sink and counter space with a couple of cupboards. There was Cole's office and a small bathroom that Ruth kept so clean the guys seemed scared to use it.

Bo had ordered a desk for himself from an office-supply store in Marquette that he'd had delivered. He'd set it up right outside her office window that she kept open so they could talk freely without having to get up from their desks.

He offered her a steaming mug of coffee with a little cream. "Ready to update the company website?"

"Yes." Ruth looked forward to this. She'd been after Cole for years to let her do something with it, but he'd put her off too many times to count.

Ruth reached for the cup, and her fingers touched Bo's hand. His skin exuded warmth and life.

He jerked back, causing the coffee to splash. "Sorry."

She grabbed a tissue and dabbed at the spilled liquid. "No harm done."

Liar.

The tips of her fingers tingled, and the sting of guilt lingered over that small spark from simply touching his skin. This wasn't good. She stole a peek at Bo, but he didn't appear to notice anything amiss, so she relaxed.

He pulled a chair around and sat next to her. "We can update the site we have or create a completely new one. It's up to you."

Having him sit close, she could just detect that clean, woodsy scent of his, and all thoughts of business scattered from her head. She focused on the laptop. "I set up the original web page, so I'm pretty familiar with the program."

He nodded. "We need pictures that reflect our services clearly as well as an estimate request."

"Right here on Cole's phone." Ruth pulled the charged cell out of her desk. She swiped the screen and tapped on the photo gallery. She'd downloaded anything personal to her home computer months ago. "Here's pictures of various jobs."

Bo took the phone and scrolled through several photos of the firewood process, tree trimming, residential-tree removal and clear-cutting. "Looks like Cole planned on updating."

Ruth nodded. "I'd been after him to do it for a while."

"He listened." Bo's expression softened.

She got lost in his eyes until the space around them seemed to shrink. Taking the phone back, she plugged it into the laptop. She needed distance; she needed absolution.

"I'll get started on this while you talk to Frank about the job schedule today."

"Holler if you need anything."

"You know I will." Ruth looked up in time to catch Bo's crooked smile. She gave Frank a wave as he made his way to the coffeepot.

She had no idea how to insert a page where a customer could request a quote, but she had lots to do before she needed help with that. Signing in to the website program, Ruth got to work amid the chatter of the guys filling up on coffee and discussing the jobs for the day.

It wasn't long before the office grew quiet again. And the smell of fresh coffee teased her nose. She looked up and spotted Bo heading for his desk with a steaming mug.

"I thought you'd left with Frank."

"I've got some paperwork to look through."

That was news to her. "What kind of paperwork?"

"Last year's tax returns."

"Oh." Ruth got up and fetched a fresh cup of coffee, then stopped at his desk. "What are you looking for?"

"We're going to need someone with a forestry background. I need to know if payroll can support someone full-time or if we only have room for one on a contractual basis."

Cole had been the one with the forestry license. "What about Frank?"

"Not the right education skill set. If we can get into the Hiawatha National Forest stewardship program, it won't be as big an issue, as they have their own forestry agents."

"Did you follow up with Cole's contact?"

Bo nodded. "I've left messages. I've also talked to a guy I grew up with who is a new forestry technician in Gladstone."

"That's good." Ruth hoped they got a call back from one of them.

"He's still getting settled into his role, but..." Bo hesitated.

"But what?"

"I'm going to meet with him at my mother's church in Toivola next Saturday."

"What's going on there?"

"It's a traditional Finn thing. There's a dinner and afterward a remembrance of loved ones lost. I'd like you to go with me and meet this guy. He might have questions about the history of the business that you'd be better equipped to answer."

Ruth considered the offer. She wasn't sure exactly where Toivola was located but knew it wasn't far from the Houghton-Hancock area of the Keweenaw Peninsula. Cole had gone to college in Houghton, and that was a good two-and-a-half-hour drive northwest of Pine.

They'd be gone a good portion of the day, maybe all day. Spending a whole Saturday away from her kids didn't feel right. Leaving Nora to referee the candy consumption from their church's harvest party wasn't right at all. Her boys could be brutal when it came to candy.

"Is it fancy?"

"Not at all. It's a potluck, but you don't have to bring a thing. There's always more than enough."

She nodded. "I'll go if my boys can come with us."

"Of course." He looked relieved.

Maybe he didn't relish spending the day alone with her either. And that smarted. A little. "Then it's a date. Er, no, not a *date*." Ruth made a face. "Sorry, I'm making this worse. We will go."

Bo chuckled. "Good. How's the website?"

Grateful to get back on normal footing, Ruth shifted gears. "Almost done, with the exception of inserting an estimate-request page. I'm not sure what I'm doing there."

"I can take a look."

Bo followed her into Cole's office—it was her office now. She had to get used to this business as hers now. Her office, her new life. She refreshed the computer screen, then stepped back so Bo could have a seat while he looked through it.

He did so at a leisurely pace, taking time to really look at each page. "I think you can do it right here, making the form with this."

Ruth watched as he clicked on the spot and proceeded to make an estimate request. "Wow. Easier than I thought."

"You can pretty it up by adding the logo." Bo got up from the chair.

Ruth considered the single pine tree they used a bit bland. "Maybe we can update the logo as well."

"Whatever you want to do." Bo didn't appear too concerned with the marketing side of things.

"Maybe another time. I want to put some thought into it." Ruth slipped into her chair, still warm from where Bo had been. "Thanks for your help."

He turned toward her. "That's what I'm here for."

Ruth considered his statement, and her conversation with Maddie and Erica rang through her thoughts. He'd turned his life upside down to help her. Was it as simple as that, or was there another reason for his help? The trust fund? Perhaps… But then, she had a feeling there was something he wasn't telling her. A lot, actually, like why he'd ended up working for Cole when he was a Harris.

Maybe a trip to his hometown and meeting his mother might give her more clues into who exactly Boothe Harris was.

"Ready?" Bo finally started his truck. He'd waited while Ruth gathered her boys along with sippy cups and fruit snacks and gadgets to keep them busy on the nearly two-and-a-half-hour drive to his mother's.

"Ready." Ruth glanced at her two boys in the back seat.

"Let's go," Owen said with a giggle.

Bo looked in the rearview mirror. Ethan was buckled into a backless booster he didn't need. The lanky kid was too big for it, in Bo's opinion. Owen, of course, had the more traditional child seat, complete with crumbs.

He'd vacuum his truck the next time he filled up with gas rather than have Ruth catch him. Bo couldn't take the apologies he'd hear. Kids made messes. He was learning that fact pretty well.

Ruth had apologized profusely when Ethan had accidentally spray-painted part of the tailgate of his truck earlier in the week. It had been a mild day, so Bo knocked off a little early from work to rent a paint sprayer to finish the picket fence. He let Ethan handle the last coat on the portion that ran between the house and garage. The next thing he knew, his black paint job had a white streak. The look on Ethan's face proved he hadn't done it on purpose, so Bo couldn't scold him.

Ruth had, though.

Ethan had been embarrassed, but he hadn't crumbled. Even after Bo had told them the paint would wash off, Ruth made Ethan help scrub. And that hadn't earned Bo any points with the eight-year-old.

Bo pulled out of the drive and gave Nora a wave.

"What's Grandma going to do?" Owen asked.

Ruth grinned. "Anything she wants."

Bo chuckled. It'd be late when they returned.

Silence soon settled over the inside of the cab, and it remained quiet even as they exited the outskirts of Pine. Tempted to turn on the radio to pass the time, Bo noticed that both the boys and Ruth stared out their respective windows.

There wasn't much to see since the leaves had all dropped, leaving stark-naked tree branches stretched against a clear blue sky. It was chilly but otherwise a fine day.

"Ooh, look! A deer." Ruth pointed.

The doe dashed back through the thick cover of bare trees.

They needed something to make the outing go faster than this. "How about we play a game?"

"What kind of game?" Ethan sounded cautious.

Bo scratched his head. He could think of only Slug Bug, and there wasn't much traffic, let alone a bunch of Volkswagen Beetles in this neck of the state.

He glanced at Ruth. "What game?"

She laughed. "How about I Spy?"

"Yeah!" Owen literally yelled.

"Ethan, you start us out." Ruth gave Bo a hopeful look.

Silence. The oldest boy wasn't as eager to take this trip as the younger one.

"I spy something that begins with the letter *A*," Ethan finally said with a sigh.

Bo scanned the horizon. Something beginning with *A*.

"ATV," Ruth blurted.

Sure enough, an all-terrain vehicle zoomed down a trail along the side of the road to turn back into the woods.

"Your turn, Mom." Owen kicked his legs against the seat.

Ruth grimaced. "Easy back there. This isn't our car." Then she rubbed her hands together and looked around. "I spy something that begins with the letter *B*."

Bo checked his rearview mirror. A school bus wasn't too far behind them. "Is it a bus?"

Ruth laughed. "It is. And it's your turn."

They played for quite a while until they got stuck on the letter *P*. Which prompted the boys to chorus for a new game.

Bo conceded that I Spy had reached a natural end. He remembered a game he used to play in grade school with the very guy they were going to see. "Would you rather be a bird or fish?"

Owen giggled. "A bird so I could fly up high in the sky."

"That's dumb," Ethan snarled.

"Is not!"

"Is too."

"Boys, come on. We've got a long way to go yet," Ruth intervened.

After a short silence, Owen piped up. "Would you rather be a mustache or a stick?"

Bo burst out laughing. "What? Where'd you get that?"

Owen giggled. And even Ethan snorted a little.

"Well, which would you rather be?" Ruth's golden eyes glowed with mirth. She wore a little makeup and her hair in loose waves.

Bo was struck again by her natural beauty, but he really needed to give his answer. After thinking about it a moment, he said, "I'd rather be a stick."

"Why?" Ethan prompted with real interest.

"So I could be thrown for fetch or used to build a fire."

"Good one." Ruth applauded.

"Wish we had a dog," Ethan muttered.

Bo glanced at Ruth. The light had gone out of her eyes. A sore spot for sure because of her allergies.

"Do you like dogs?" Owen asked.

"I love dogs. Growing up, my grandfather kept border collies to help manage the sheep that he raised." Once Bo had gone to work for his father, he traveled too much to have a pet.

"Me too," Owen said with pride, as if glad for something in common.

That shining agreement did something to Bo. It pulled on his heart in a way he wasn't accustomed to. He'd never gone on a road trip with his parents. He'd never had siblings to argue with either. He had a stepsister and stepbrother, but they were twelve and fifteen years younger than him. They'd never been close.

Road trips were what families did together. Something he'd missed out on. And that realization left him wanting more of these outings with Ruth and her boys. They'd become his secret family in a way. Maybe he wanted more than just a marriage deal, but was that even possible?

Glancing at Ruth with her sad eyes, he doubted it. She was in love with her dead husband and rightly so. The attraction he felt for her was growing, but even if she made room in her heart for him, anything they might have would be crushed by the knowledge that he may have had a hand in Cole's death.

For both their sakes, and that of the boys, he'd keep to the agreement they'd made. This legal union was a business deal, and that's all it could ever be.

Chapter Nine

As they drove past the post office, which was heartbreakingly small, Ruth turned to Bo. "So, this is like only four corners."

He chuckled. "Toivola is more of an area than a village."

"Cole and his brother used to come up here to snowmobile," Ruth said.

"The Keweenaw Peninsula has a lot of trails. And old copper mines and pristine Lake Superior shoreline."

"How far are we from Michigan Tech? That's where Cole went to college for forestry."

Bo took a couple of quick turns and ended up on a dirt road. "About fifteen miles or so. My mom recently retired from Finlandia University, which is just over the bridge in Hancock. She made the commute easily enough."

Ruth remembered that the two college towns were connected by the Portage Lake Lift Bridge.

The last time she'd been there with Cole, they'd picnicked at a park near that bridge. They'd spent the afternoon watching it lift and close, marveling at the boats that passed underneath. It had been one of many perfect days in their lives.

Ruth sat forward as Bo pulled into a two-track drive that led to a pretty yellow farmhouse with blue shutters and flower boxes. The flower boxes were filled with evergreen and pumpkins. A whitewashed barn stood farther back on a property that looked endless.

A tall, attractive woman dressed in jeans and an Icelandic-style sweater stood on the porch, waiting for Bo to park.

Ruth noticed the resemblance immediately when Bo's mom approached the truck. She had the same icy blue-gray eyes as her son.

"Boothe." His mom drew him close for a hug. "Oh my, you need a haircut."

Bo chuckled. "I work in the woods. Nobody cares what my hair looks like."

"But you look like a vagrant." His mother gave him a teasing shove before turning toward Ruth with a broad smile. "Welcome. I'm Anja Tervonen."

The lilt in her voice hinted at a slight accent.

Ruth extended her hand. "Ruth Miller, and these two—" she corralled the boys close "—are my sons, Ethan and Owen."

"How do you do. Come in, come in and relax. We've got some time before Pyhäinpäivä."

"Wait, say that again so I can give it a try." Ruth loved the sound of the word, even though she'd never remember how to pronounce it.

"Poo-han-peye-va." Bo's mom had spoken very slowly.

Feeling confident, Ruth gave it a try. "Poo-hanpeyeva."

His mom's smile was wide and warm. "Very good."

"We didn't bring a dish to pass." Ruth wrinkled her nose.

"No need." Anja waved her hand in dismissal. "I have made plenty of *karjalanpiirakka.*"

Ruth looked at Bo for interpretation. There was no way she'd attempt that one.

"It's a rice-filled pastry, and they're pretty good."

"Sounds interesting." They certainly smelled good. The aroma coming from Anja's kitchen made her mouth water.

After taking their coats and laying them on the couch, Bo's mom leaned toward the boys. "Are you hungry? We can all try one now."

Ethan nodded, but Owen played shy and hid behind Ruth's leg.

"I'd love to try one." Ruth had to find out if they tasted as good as they smelled.

"Come." Anja headed for the kitchen.

In no time, they were seated at a large wooden table in the center of a real farmhouse kitchen while Anja doled out the goodies. Ruth split one in half for the boys. The pastries were oval in shape, with a darker crust than she'd expected. A small crock of some very yellow-looking egg salad was set on the table as well.

"*Munavoi.* Egg butter," Anja explained.

Ruth shrugged, dipped her knife in and slathered her pastry, then took a bite. It wasn't exactly sweet or savory but really good and hearty, like something eaten for a cold winter's breakfast. "Delicious."

Anja smiled at her son. "She has good taste, I see."

Ruth nearly laughed when color crept up Bo's neck.

He turned to Ethan. "Do you like it?"

Ethan reached for the egg butter and spread a little on his half. "It's okay, I guess."

Ruth watched as Owen waited for Bo to finish his before taking a bite. He chewed as if considering the taste, then went in for a second bite. No egg butter for him. Owen had decided he didn't like eggs these days and was sticking to it.

"Good, huh?" Ruth prodded her youngest.

Owen nodded and kept eating.

Anja checked her watch. "Okay, time for me to pack these up and go. I'm on the committee, so I need to be early. You can come a little later. Bo, dinner starts at five."

"We'll be there."

"Can I help?" Ruth started to get up.

Anja waved away her offer. "Sit, sit and enjoy. I've got this."

Ruth raised her plate. "Thank you for these."

Bo's mom smiled. "You're so welcome."

It didn't take Anja long to exit the house. Ruth glanced at the clock. They still had half an hour before they had to leave. Ruth took her plate to the deep sink, where she rinsed it, ready to put it in the dishwasher—only there wasn't one.

Whoa. Ruth would definitely struggle without hers. It appeared that Anja could afford a dishwasher if she wanted one, so she preferred washing her own dishes. That was definitely old-school.

"Just leave it in the sink," Bo said.

"No way. I can wash it." Ruth looked underneath for dish soap and went to work.

Bo brought his plate over. Ethan and Owen were still at the table, eating.

"So, your mom is like *really* Finnish." Ruth rinsed the plates and set them in the strainer.

Bo laughed. "Both my maternal grandparents emigrated from Finland. They met here and married, but had only my mom."

"How'd she meet your father?"

Bo leaned against the counter. "My dad was

up here on business, and they met at some chamber of commerce event in Hancock. They never married, even though my father asked. My mom wouldn't leave the area or her parents, who were already in their sixties when I was born."

Ruth frowned at the matter-of-fact way Bo had rattled off that information. His eyes shone more blue than gray today, but the iciness seemed harder. As usual, he gave no hint to the emotions that might be trapped inside; but still, he seemed more open here than back home in Pine. For that small peek into Bo Harris, she was glad she'd come.

"Mom." Owen tugged on her sweater. "I have to go to the bathroom."

"Okay." Ruth had to go as well. "Where it is?"

"Near the front entry, by the stairs," Bo said.

Ruth took Owen's hand and walked through the dining room, marveling at pictures of who must be Bo's grandparents. Garden shots and photographs of the family shearing sheep and gathering around a Christmas tree were all lovingly framed and grouped along one wall. There was even a photo of a very young Bo with his grandfather. To Ruth's horror, both were holding chain saws. Wasn't there a law about kids under sixteen using motorized equipment?

"Mom…" Owen tugged again.

"Okay." She hurried into the foyer and opened

the door beneath the stairs that led to a small powder room.

Leaving the door open but giving Owen his space, Ruth stepped back to view photos of Bo as a child that littered the wall of the stairway. He'd been a towheaded blond with a carefree expression that changed into something much more solemn as he grew older.

Bo was handsome in his black cap and gown as he stood next to a shorter man who must be his father, Robert Harris. High school or college, Ruth couldn't tell, but Mr. Harris beamed with pride while Bo's smile looked forced, as if they didn't get along. Maybe they'd had a falling-out, and that's why Bo left his father's employ. It would have been a doozy of a disagreement to part ways. Maybe she should ask.

Ruth checked on Owen, made sure he washed his hands and then used the facility before joining Bo and Ethan back in the kitchen—only, they weren't in the kitchen. Ruth looked out the window over the sink and spotted them outside near the barn.

She grabbed Owen by the hand and went outside. Standing on the bottom step of the porch, she watched Bo and Ethan chase a bunch of chickens. The two laughed until, finally, they each caught one.

"Mom, look. Aren't they cool?" Ethan stood next to Bo and held a reddish-feathered hen.

Bo was holding a big black-and-white one.

Her son's wide smile made her heart skip. "Yes, Ethan. They are really cool."

"Mr. Harris let me catch her all by myself."

"I saw that." Ruth glanced at Bo and smiled. The man knew his way into her son's heart. And that small gesture was making its way into hers too.

What Ruth thought was really cool, was the chatter between Ethan and Bo about those chickens on the short drive to Anja's church.

Dinner had been enjoyable, with traditional Finnish dishes Bo could hardly pronounce alongside regular fare. The minister had prayed over the food and then mentioned the names of church members who had died the previous year. He asked the congregation to keep the families in their prayers for comfort.

He'd been to several of these gatherings while growing up. He'd found them boring in the past, but not tonight. Tonight held new meaning for him as he reminisced over his own losses. Bo kept thinking about his grandfather and Cole, and how much he missed both men.

After dinner, a kids' program kept Ethan and Owen busy while he caught up with Janet's son Rick. He was the new forest technician, and their conversation had been fruitful. They'd even reminisced about their time in grade school together, all while Ruth chatted with his mom.

"I'll pass your name and number to the forest supervisor and let him know you'd like to offer a bid." Rick pocketed the generic Miller Logging and Tree Service business card with Bo's cell phone number written alongside the office number.

"Thanks, Rick. I look forward to the opportunity." They might have a chance. Slim, but a chance nonetheless.

"Yeah, sure. Take care." Rick walked away.

Bo glanced at Ruth, but she was still locked in an animated conversation with his mom. Neither one noticed him as he approached. "Are we ready to light the candles?"

Ruth tipped her head. "What candles?"

"As the minister mentioned, Pyhäinpäivä is a Finnish custom of remembering those who've passed. We honor our loved ones by lighting candles that are placed at their gravesites," his mom explained before Bo could.

"Oh, that's a lovely custom." Ruth smiled.

"My grandparents are buried here in the cemetery behind the church. You don't have to join us. You and the boys can stay inside, if you prefer." He hadn't considered that this part of the evening might be a sad reminder for her.

"I'd like to watch, if I may."

"Of course." He was okay with that, but for some reason, having Ruth join in made him feel awfully exposed.

Bundled up, Ruth stood back, holding Ethan's and Owen's hands on either side of her. The candles were white votives placed in small jars. Some people lingered at gravesites after lighting them, while others did not. There was a cold nip in the air now that the sun had set, but it wasn't quite dark yet. The glow of candles scattered about the little cemetery seemed more peaceful than spooky.

As a believer, Ruth knew the souls of those buried here were not in the ground. This custom wasn't for the dead but the living who were left behind. Thinking of Cole, and how much she hated visiting his grave, she knew she needed to do this very same thing with the boys. And Nora. It might help give a little more closure, honoring Cole's memory with a candle.

She watched as Anja held two candles inside jars for Bo to light. Neither said a word as Anja placed the flickering lights on either side of her parents' headstones. The names *Kalle Boothe Tervonen* and *Aada Kaarina Tervonen* were deeply etched, along with their dates of birth and death.

"That's it." Rather than linger, Anja rose and clapped her hands together once, as if ready to move on to her next duty. Then she pointed toward the woods. "It's a beautiful night for a walk, if you'd like to follow the lighted trail."

"Oh, how pretty. I'd love to go." Ruth turned her attention back to the gravesite and caught Bo giving his grandfather's headstone a gentle caress. The simple gesture tore at her heart.

Bo had also known loss in his life. His mother had told her about a broken engagement five years ago that had nearly destroyed him. And that's about when he'd left Harris Industries.

"Can we?" Ethan asked.

Ruth looked at Bo. He'd driven them there, and she didn't know how long he wanted to stay. "Will a walk make it too late getting back?"

He shrugged. "Not at all."

"Wonderful." Anja waved them on. "Go enjoy."

"Aren't you coming with us?" Ruth asked.

Anja smiled. "No. I'm going to help clean up with some friends."

Ruth had monopolized Bo's mom through dinner and dessert, but the woman was so warm and easy to talk to. Anja had told Ruth quite a bit, including how happy she was that Bo had moved back to the Upper Peninsula.

"Mom, if you leave before we get back, we'll stop at the house to say goodbye."

"Very good." Anja waved again as she darted into the church.

"Let's go." Ethan ran toward the path with Owen hot on his brother's heels.

"Nothing dangerous ahead, is there?" Ruth eyed the woodchip-strewn path lit with paper luminaires.

Bo gave her a disarming grin. "On the trail, no."

"Then where?" Ruth teased back.

Bo answered quickly. "We've got a year to figure that out."

Ruth laughed, but her stomach flipped. Talk about a loaded statement. She glanced at his profile. Bo looked more relaxed than she'd ever seen him. Not that she'd known him long enough or well enough to really know.

Needing a subject change, she asked, "Do you speak Finnish?"

He shrugged. "Not much. I used to understand some, could read a little of it, but I'm pretty rusty when it comes to speech."

"Would you say something?" Ruth was definitely curious.

He pondered a moment, rubbing the stubble on his chin before saying, *"Me ollaan ystäviä."*

Ruth grinned, loving the foreign sound of his voice. "What's it mean?"

"We are friends."

"Are we?" She'd let that slip out before thinking.

He looked at her longer than a second or two. "I hope so."

Another little shiver went through her. "I hope so too."

That felt too awkward, so Ruth added yet another question. "You said that you've traveled to Finland. Do they speak English?"

"Yes. It's common over there, so I didn't have to try too hard."

"I bet it's beautiful."

"I've only been to the capital, Helsinki, but yeah, it was a beautiful city, right on the Baltic Sea. Old and all that."

Ruth could only imagine what it might be like to travel to a foreign country. She hadn't even been to Canada, and that wasn't very far away. She sank her hands into her pockets to keep them warm. It was a clear night for the first Saturday in November, and the temperature had dropped after a sun-filled afternoon.

The boys ran ahead of them on the path.

"Warm enough?" Bo's hands were also deep in his pockets.

"Yes." Ruth considered the evening as a whole and was glad they'd come. Glad for the chance to see this side of him. "Were you close to your grandfather?"

Bo nodded. "I was."

"Can I ask you something?"

"Now I see where Owen gets it." Bo chuckled. "Of course. You can ask me anything you like."

Ruth made a face. "How old were you when you learned how to use a chain saw?"

Bo tipped his head. "Why?"

"At your mother's, there is a picture of you and your grandfather with chain saws. You don't look much older than Ethan."

"I think I was eleven when he taught me to use the small one."

"That's awfully young."

Bo shrugged. "Things were different then. My grandfather made sure I knew what to do and didn't let me out of his sight."

The wooded path suddenly emptied into a clearing, complete with a roaring campfire. Folks sat on logs around the fire, and someone handed out cups of something hot.

"Cider?" Bo asked Ruth.

"Yes, please. This is really nice." She reached for a cup. Her boys stood watching the fire, their faces aglow from the flames.

"The walking path is a new thing." Bo lifted his cup. "The cider too. I don't know, maybe they are trying to attract more folks. More families."

A walk like this was too romantic by far to come alone. But she wasn't looking for romance. Although, she was grateful that Bo considered them friends.

She peered up into a sky filled with stars and a bright crescent moon. Without lights from houses and a town, the multitude of stars was truly awesome. Humbling too.

She silently thanked God for this special night and the custom she'd like to repeat at Cole's grave. It might be good for the boys since they hadn't been to the cemetery since Cole's funeral.

"Beautiful night," Bo said.

"It is. Thank you for bringing us here."

"Thanks for coming." Bo reached for her empty cup and tossed it in the fire along with his. "Ready to head back?"

She wasn't really, but what else was there to do or see? The boys looked antsy as well. They were throwing woodchips from the path into the woods. "Sure. Come on, boys. Time to head home."

Ethan threw one more woodchip before running past them, careening out of the way of another couple coming down the path into the clearing.

Ruth shook her head. At least he was enjoying himself. He hadn't wanted to come.

Owen didn't rush away; he stayed with them. "Is this yours?"

"What? The woods?"

Owen nodded.

"Nope. It belongs to my mother's church. My church, too, when I was a kid."

"Will you go to our church tomorrow?"

"Uh…" Ruth wasn't sure about that. What if

he sat with them? Everyone would wonder who he was and— Shame on her. It shouldn't matter what people thought.

She looked at Bo. "It's a nice church."

"Sorry, Owen, but I have my own church to attend." Bo gave her a wink, obviously picking up on the reason for her hesitation. "It's the one down the road from the office."

Ruth knew the one. A small congregation, more traditional and yet a very nice church. "How long have you gone there?"

"A few months," Bo said.

Owen slipped his little hand into Bo's. "Come on, Mr. Harris. Let's race."

"Owen…" Ruth tried to intervene, but Bo had already agreed, and off the two went.

It was a bittersweet sight, reminding her of how good a father Cole had been. Was it fair for Bo to fill part of the void? What if her sons grew too attached? And what about her?

And that's when Ruth found herself asking God to keep her and her boys safe because Bo had been right when he'd teased earlier. There were all kinds of danger ahead of them.

Bo pulled into his mom's driveway. "I'll just be a minute."

"Of course. Take your time."

"Are you sure you don't want to come in?"

Bo noticed that Ruth had been quiet on the walk back to the church. Real quiet.

"The boys are settled down and maybe they'll—" she mouthed the word *sleep* "—on the way home."

"I'm wide awake," Ethan said with a yawn.

Bo chuckled. The kid might be asleep by the time he climbed back in the truck. He left it running, with the heat blasting.

"Thanks. Tell your mom it was nice meeting her."

Bo nodded and ran toward the house, taking the porch steps two at a time. Entering the home where he'd spent his tender years, he found his mother in the kitchen. She looked tired but content. His mother had always found contentment in her life.

He wrapped his arms around her. "Thank you."

"Of course. I like Ruth. She's more down-to-earth than that other woman."

"Sheri?" Bo chuckled. His mom didn't like saying her name.

"Yes, her. I never did care for her. She was too fussy."

In hindsight, Bo had dodged a bullet there. "Ruth and I are just business partners. I bought into her late husband's business. He was the guy I told you about that died in the field."

His mother stepped back. "Oh, Boothe, I'm sorry. That was only this summer."

"Yes."

His mom patted his hand. "Don't let her get away. She's good for you, and those boys are too."

How could she even know? "Mom—"

"Listen, the heart is big enough for two loves in a lifetime."

Bo narrowed his gaze. His father had moved on and married another, but his mother never had. "It wasn't for you."

She waved her hand in dismissal. "That was different. I wasn't a Christian back then. I made choices that might not have been the best, but I had your grandparents and my job. My place has always been here."

"Perhaps I'll make the same choice."

His mother cupped his cheek. "Please don't. You're lonely. I see it."

He couldn't deny that.

She patted his shoulder and then pushed a foil-wrapped plate into his hands.

"What's this?"

"Sugar cookies."

His favorite. He kissed his mom's cheek. "Love you."

"Love you, too, son. Be safe."

"I will."

He planned on being safe. Especially after

teasing Ruth. He'd been surprised when she'd teased right back. When she'd asked if they were friends, he'd had a hard time answering correctly. He wanted more than friendship, but that was not part of their deal.

He climbed into his truck, setting the foil plate on the console between them. Sure enough, both of the Miller boys were conked out in their seats. He and Ruth waved to his mom standing on the porch as he drove off.

"There's sugar cookies under that foil, if you'd like one."

"Thank you, but I'm stuffed from dinner." Ruth leaned her seat back a little.

"You joining your boys?" He knew how well she could sleep in the passenger seat.

"Me? No. I'm wide awake." She yawned, just like Ethan.

They both laughed. And then silence settled in.

Until Ruth piped up with yet another question. "Can I ask you something?"

"Sure." Bo braced for it.

"Why haven't you ever married?"

He considered giving her a pat comment but thought better of it. "I got close once. Real close."

"What happened?" Ruth shifted in her seat so that she sort of faced him. She looked ready for a story.

But how much to tell? If he explained that Sheri was only after his trust fund, he'd slam Ruth, even though it had been his idea to get married.

"If it's too painful—" she whispered.

He let out a short bark of a laugh. The pain had subsided years ago, leaving behind a dullness inside that he didn't like to examine too closely. "It's not that. We worked together at Harris Industries. She was the head of marketing, and we dated for a while. Then we were engaged for a while. It took me too long to figure out that she loved what came with being Mrs. Harris. It wasn't me she was really after."

Ruth bit her lip, reading between the lines of what he said and didn't say. Still, Ruth looked like she knew exactly what he'd meant. "Is that why you quit working for your father?"

He let out a sigh. "Part of the reason, yeah. She's still there."

"And the other part?" Ruth asked softly.

He kept his gaze firmly fixed on the road, scanning the sides for deer or anything else that might pop out of the woods. "It wasn't what I wanted anymore. Flipping businesses for profit is a cruel way to make a living. I realized that I'd ordered one too many layoffs and closures under the guise of 'restructuring.'"

Ruth winced at the hollow sound in his voice. "Your father must have been disappointed."

"That's an understatement. He wanted me to take it all over one day. He'd been grooming me for it since I was a teen, with a private high school and then college and grad school. At least living here feels right."

"You can take the man out of the UP, but you can't take the UP out of the man," Ruth said with a smile.

"That's true." Bo laughed.

He'd never considered that saying, but it was certainly true for him. Buying that fifty acres of land had been the beginning of the end for him at Harris Industries.

"So, if not you, who will run it?" Ruth asked.

He shrugged. "Maybe my stepsister or stepbrother."

She looked surprised. "I didn't know you had siblings. You never mention them. Are you not close?"

"No. Not really. I'm a good fifteen years older than them. When I wasn't away at school, or interning at Harris Industries most of the summer, I was with my mom during holidays."

Ruth smiled. "I really like your mom."

Bo looked at Ruth. "She liked you as well. You two had lots to talk about."

"Yes."

At that tight-lipped response, Bo wondered how much of the conversation had included him. Egocentric, perhaps, but his mother wasn't above highlighting his qualities to single females she liked.

He considered what his mom had said about choices and making room in his heart for another. He'd considered that possibility with Ruth, and it made sense. He liked her, found her attractive and he had time to pursue her. A whole year stretched ahead of them.

But what if Ruth's heart remained closed? She might choose to remain alone like his mother had. And that would be a real shame.

Chapter Ten

Despite the sharp dip in temperatures, Pine had seen little snow in the last two weeks. This morning, Ruth made her way into work before sunrise, hoping to catch Bo, who made a habit of going in early. Getting out of her minivan, she pulled the collar of her down coat closer and shivered. Her breath made puffs of mist in the below-freezing air as she walked.

Looking around the lot, she saw a thick layer of frost that covered the ground and hung on the distant trees that made the place look sleepy in the soft morning light. This quiet would soon fade when the crews arrived and filled the air with sounds of idling trucks and shouted directions. November had proved to be busy due to losing one of their woodcutters to a competitor and new business rolling in.

Once inside the building, Ruth hung up her coat, then stepped into her office to turn on the little space heater under her desk. Dressed in flannel-lined jeans and a turtleneck with a thick fleece sweatshirt, she was still cold. "I'd rather it snow if it's going to be this cold."

"Supposed to this week." Bo entered with a cup of coffee for her in his hand. "I think I might have a buyer for Cole's truck."

Ruth stopped midreach. "Yeah?"

"Are you sure you want to sell it?" Bo's expression softened.

She grabbed the coffee he offered, wrapping both hands around the warm porcelain mug. "Yes, I'm sure."

Ruth needed to let the truck go. She needed to let go of Cole too. Erica and Maddie had agreed when they'd had lunch the previous week. Especially after she'd told them about the Finnish custom she'd recreated at Cole's gravesite with Nora and the boys. One day after school, they'd gone with votive candles and jars in hand. It hadn't been easy.

Nora had cried when Owen talked to the ground as if he could speak to his dad. Ethan had informed his brother that their dad wasn't really there; he was in Heaven with God. Owen didn't fully understand but had nodded, believing Ethan's gentle words.

Ruth's heart had been broken but full. Despite the emotional afternoon, a milestone had been reached. Acceptance of Cole's death had wrapped them in a blanket of comfort. Cole was gone, and as much as they missed him, he was in a good place. A better place.

"Here's the guy's name and number. I can be there if you want me to be."

"Thank you for that, but I can do it." Ruth took the paper and stared at it.

Bo had helped establish the price range; then he'd started the truck, pulled it out onto the lawn and placed a for-sale sign in the window with the office phone number. She needed to take care of the rest of it on her own. More closure.

She felt Bo give her shoulder a quick squeeze and looked up. But he'd already moved on, around to his desk, while reviewing the printed estimate requests that she'd received through Miller Logging and Tree Service's updated website.

It had been a comforting gesture and nothing more. Not that she wanted more. She didn't. Not really.

"Hey, these are some great estimate requests. Frank and I can follow up later this week."

"Good." She'd screened them pretty well, but they were similar to the others they'd received since updating the website, mostly small stuff.

He gave her a grin. "Good job with our site." *Our.*

The word rang through her ears and settled somewhere in her throat, clogging it. She squeezed her eyes shut against the tears that suddenly stung. She'd been trying to let go of Cole, but hearing Bo refer to this business as his and hers made letting go even more real and final. Cole was gone, and his business was changing.

She was changing too. More involved in the day-to-day business than ever before, Ruth experienced a sense of pride and accomplishment. Would Cole be proud?

Ruth shook off those thoughts and emotions threatening to overwhelm her and got back to the business of the day. She only had so much time before Bo headed out with one of the crews. Clearing her throat, she asked, "Any word from that forest supervisor?"

"Not yet. I don't anticipate anything until after the holidays." Bo downed the last of his coffee and headed for a refill. "Want more?"

"No, I have plenty yet." Her stomach twisted at the reminder that the holidays were bearing down fast.

Thanksgiving loomed at the end of the week, and she was barely prepared for it. She knew the first holidays were the hardest, but Ruth wanted to make this Thanksgiving-into-Christmas season a good one for her boys.

"We usually close the Friday and Saturday after Thanksgiving. I think we should do that again this year," she hollered through the open window between their desks.

"Sounds good to me." Bo returned with a steaming refill.

"Will you head to your mom's?" She cringed at the way her voice nearly cracked.

"Yeah, probably. What about you?"

Ruth shrugged. "We stay put. Me and Nora and the boys. My parents will fly in on Wednesday and stay through the weekend. They usually spend Christmas with my sister."

"Where do they live?"

"Here in the summer and Florida in the winter. My sister and her husband live in South Carolina. Easier traveling there for my parents come December."

Bo nodded, but he was focused on today's work schedule.

She had another question. "I was thinking we should up the advertising budget for next year. Not that we ever spent much, but we need to do more than sponsor restaurant place mats at the diner."

"Sure. Look into it."

The door opened and Frank, along with a couple of other guys, stepped inside. It appeared that everyone was getting an early start.

Bo turned toward her as he slouched into his coat and gloves. "Do you mind finding out how much radio spots might run?"

"I don't mind at all." She looked forward to

it. It'd give her more variety than fielding calls and following up on estimate requests.

As she watched the guys leave, she kicked herself for asking Bo like she'd needed his permission. Miller Logging and Tree Service needed to grow, and better advertising would help. Ruth had to take ownership of her position as partner and take the lead on some things. That would help her grow as well.

Bo turned down the thermostat in the apartment above Ruth's garage since he'd be gone for a few days at his mom's. The day before Thanksgiving felt festive, with light snow falling outside. He and Frank had decided to call it quits early, which made the guys happy. It gave them a chance to hit their deer blinds before dark.

Ruth had taken the day off to get ready for her parents arriving later in the evening. He was relieved he'd miss meeting them. Bo didn't think he could take the scrutiny. Parents had a way of uncovering things he tried to keep hidden— like the fact that he might be falling for his business partner.

Ruth had done a great job with the office. She'd taken over marketing and public relations all at once, it seemed. She qualified the estimate requests before sending them his way. He'd heard her on the phone, laying out the basic costs and processes. Ruth made sure folks were truly interested in having tree work done or fields cleared before handing that lead his way.

Whatever the request, Ruth saved him time making those calls. She probably sealed several potential jobs as well. There was something about the warmth in her voice that fostered trust. He'd be blind not to notice how much the people of Pine missed Cole Miller. Seeing his widow carry on in his place went a long way in getting new business as well.

After grabbing his leather duffel and briefcase, Bo headed down the stairs to his truck. Glancing at the house, he figured he'd better pop in and see if Ruth needed anything before he left.

Tossing his bags in the back seat, he headed for the side door. If he were truthful, he simply wanted to see her before leaving. He'd morphed into a lovesick teen over the last couple of weeks. Ever since he'd taken Ruth home to meet his mom. Getting away would no doubt be good for him. He needed the distance to regroup and refocus on their business agreement.

He knocked on the door, but there was no answer.

Looking around, he saw that Nora's car was gone. Maybe Ruth had gone somewhere with her. He was about to step away when he heard a thump, followed by a muffled sob. He tried the doorknob, and it opened. Entering the laundry room, he could hear sobbing somewhere inside, and his stomach dropped like a stone in a deep well.

It was Ruth.

He rushed forward, praying she hadn't hurt herself. Coming around the corner, he spotted her sitting in the middle of the living room floor. Artificial tree branches were strewn about, and the skeleton of the tree lay on the floor, too, like it had fallen over or been pushed.

Hearing him, she looked up with red-rimmed eyes and tearstained cheeks. The forsaken expression on her face sliced right through him.

Bo backed up, ready to bolt, but he couldn't leave her like this. And then he asked the dumbest question. "Do you need help with the tree?"

She sniffed and gave a wobbly sort of laugh. "I'm, uh, no. I just hate it when the color tags fall off from the branches and I have to sort by size."

He knew better than to believe that.

She stood, wiping her hands against the back side of her stretchy-looking pants. "I'm sorry. Was there anything you needed?"

An invisible thread drew him toward her. "I was going to ask you that before I left for my mom's."

She shook her head. "Nope. I'm all set."

"You're not," he whispered. "Want to talk about it?"

She shook her head again, but her eyes teared

up, and she placed her hand over her mouth as if trying to stave off another sob.

He did the only thing he could and opened his arms.

She stepped right in.

He carefully wrapped his arms around her shaking shoulders and patted her back as she gave way to a full-blown cry. He didn't say a word. He knew this was about missing Cole. About spending her first Thanksgiving without him. There was nothing he could say that might ease the pain, so he simply held her.

Closing his eyes tight against the visions of her husband lying lifeless on the ground, Bo pulled her closer. He should tell her, he knew he should, but he couldn't. Not now. Not like this. Not when he could barely explain what had happened or why.

He thought he'd fastened that pull rope correctly. He could see himself crank the come-along tight, but had he? He'd done it so many times; like any routine, it was hard to remember if he'd truly done it or not. Coward that he was, he'd never asked for verification because he dreaded hearing that his carelessness caused that tree to twist.

Ruth's sobs had subsided to sniffles, but she remained locked in his arms. Her head lay against his chest, so he stroked the red strands of her hair, relishing how silky it felt. Running his fingers through it, he measured its weight and thickness, only to slide his fingers through it all over again.

He heard her sigh and slid his hands along her shoulders, down her back to rest at her sides, spanning her waist and drawing her closer still. This wasn't about comfort anymore, and it was high time he stepped away, but—

Ruth must have felt it, too, because she suddenly jerked back and stared at him wide-eyed.

He gazed into those golden brown eyes of hers and panicked. "Ruth—"

She stumbled backward over a stack of plastic tree branches, her face ablaze. "I'm sorry."

"Don't be." He reached out to steady her, but she'd already righted herself.

He wasn't sorry. And if he didn't leave soon, he'd pull her right back into his arms and show her how not sorry he was.

Bo heard the side door open, followed by the rustling of bags.

Nora called out, "Anyone home?"

"We're in here." Ruth wiped her face with her hands as if trying to erase what had just happened between them.

Time to escape.

"Oh, Bo. I didn't know you were here."

Bo noticed that Ruth had bent down to retrieve the fallen Christmas tree. She wouldn't meet his gaze.

He turned toward Nora. "Just checking to see if you needed anything before I left for my mom's."

"I think we're all set." Nora glanced at Ruth and then back at him. "Thank you, though."

Was the hum of awareness between them that tangible? All the more reason to run now, while he could. "Okay, then. Have a good Thanksgiving."

"You too. Safe travels." Nora waved.

Bo didn't wait for Ruth's goodbye. He booked it out of there and into his truck, and was on the road before he changed his mind. Before he did something stupid, like ask Ruth if there might be a chance for them to be more than business partners.

He'd promised otherwise and needed to hold up his end for as long as required. This marriage deal was his idea and heading south fast. Time to apply the brakes.

Thanksgiving dinner had been wonderfully made by her mom and Nora. They had chased her out of the kitchen, and so here she was on cleanup duty and grateful for it. Her father and the boys watched the remainder of the Lions football game in the family room while her mother and Nora strung lights on the assembled Christmas tree in the living room. Christmas music flowed from that room, as well as her mom and mother-in-law's friendly chatter. They'd always gotten along great.

With some space to herself, Ruth could finally breathe a little. But thoughts of Bo invaded that space. She closed her eyes, and goose bumps rose on her arms as she recollected the feel of his hands in her hair and on her back.

This isn't good at all.

Their Thanksgiving Day table had a gaping hole where Cole should have been. She'd expected that, but what Ruth hadn't expected was wishing Bo had been with them. She could use a dose of his crooked smile and soft teasing.

Bo's embrace had ignited something deep within her, but any romantic feelings she thought she felt could *not* be real. She hadn't been held in four months; it was no wonder hugging him had felt so good.

She put away the leftovers, loaded the dishwasher and finished cleaning up the rest of the kitchen before joining her mom and Nora.

"Should we put on the ornaments?" Her mom stood before the tree loaded with white lights.

"Why not?" This was Ruth's favorite part of decorating the tree anyway.

She had grabbed the rest of the Christmas cheer from the attic when she'd brought down the tree. The ornament boxes were neatly stacked against the far wall, plastic bins filled with a mix of store-bought treasures and homemade ornaments she'd created with her boys.

In the past, Ruth had put up their artificial tree

with only white lights the day before Thanksgiving. Then they'd decorate the rest of it as a family the following night. There didn't seem to be a reason to keep that tradition going without Cole. He'd been the one who'd suggested it because he'd loved watching them hang the ornaments and plastic icicles, pointing out the holes or a lopsided strand of garland.

Shame filled Ruth as she stared at the tree. How could she be attracted to Bo and miss her dead husband in practically the same breath?

"I'll make us hot chocolate." Nora scurried off toward the kitchen.

Her mom touched her arm, giving it a gentle rub. "How are you?"

It was hard putting on a front with her own mother, but Ruth didn't want to drag anyone down. The boys had been happy to see their grandparents, and Ruth wanted to keep that happiness going for as long as possible.

"I'm okay," Ruth finally said.

"Nora says a relative stepped in to save Cole's business."

Good ole Nora. At least she didn't use the Boaz line on her mom. Not that her mom would know the Old Testament story. Her parents didn't share Ruth's faith. "Cole's second cousin. He worked with Cole, and now he's helping me."

"Good. At least you have your dental hygienist experience to fall back on if things don't work out."

Ruth wasn't about to inform her mom that it wouldn't be easy going back to dental work after all these years. "It'll work out."

It had to. She'd signed an agreement. Their marriage deal had included an annulment at the end of a year, which meant no emotional attachments. She had to honor that. They were friends. Friends helped each other. That's all it was. Despite the electricity of that embrace, she was going to act normal come Monday morning.

She'd been grieving and vulnerable. If Bo was half the man she hoped he was, he'd understand that. He shouldn't even bring it up. They simply had to forget that anything had occurred between them. Other than a comforting embrace, nothing *had* happened.

Her phone dinged with an incoming text. Glancing at it, Ruth's stomach flipped. It was Bo. With an unsteady hand, she tapped the message to open it. She smiled at the photo he'd sent with a Happy Thanksgiving emoji and message to Ethan.

Tell Ethan his hen finally laid eggs.

"Ethan, come here a minute."
Her mom leaned in for a peek. "Who's that?"
She played it casual. "That's the relative who's

helping with Miller Logging and his mom, Anja."

"What?" Ethan came toward her.

Ruth turned the phone so her son could see the selfie of Bo holding the red hen while Anja held four perfect eggs with light green shells.

Ethan's eyes lit up. "Wow, cool! Can we go back there sometime?"

"Maybe." Ruth couldn't make any promises. They'd have to be invited.

"When were you there?" Ruth's mom probed.

Ruth might have opened a hornet's nest by letting her mother see that photo. "A few weeks ago. We met with a forest technician about a job lead. The boys came along, and we visited Bo's mom."

"She has chickens, and I got to hold the red one," Ethan explained.

"Well, that must have been special." There was a definite question in her mom's eyes.

"It was great." Ethan turned to examine the ornament boxes. "Are we decorating the tree?"

"Yes. Ethan, see if your brother wants to help, and tell Grandpa what we're doing in case he wants to join us."

Ethan dashed off to comply.

"You're pretty friendly with this man if you've met his mother."

Ruth shook her head. "It was her church where we met the forest tech."

Her mother's eyebrows shot up.

Ruth knew she wasn't going to leave it alone. "We're friends, Mom. He's buying into Cole's business, and that's all it is."

"Huh." Her mother accepted the answer, but Ruth knew this wasn't the end of it.

"Hot chocolate!" Nora entered, holding a tray of mugs topped with whipped cream and chocolate shavings.

Ruth had never been so glad to escape her mother's inquiry. "Thanks, Nora. Let's decorate."

Moments later, they were all together, decorating the Christmas tree, with music and hot chocolate and laughter. It felt good and it felt right, even though Ruth found herself glancing at the couch, remembering Cole and the many holidays they'd shared.

As the evening wound down into nightfall, Ruth changed into her pajamas and climbed into bed. It had been a long day but a good one. She grabbed her phone and opened up the text from Bo with the picture of the red hen. Part of her desperately wanted to call him, but she knew better. It was nearly ten o'clock.

She opted to text him instead. Thank you for sending that picture. Ethan loved it.

It wasn't long before he texted back. You're welcome. How'd you do today?

She smiled. He understood the sadness

Thanksgiving had brought her. Although Nora struggled through similar emotions, Ruth couldn't lay her burdens down on her mother-in-law today. They kept each other afloat by keeping it light for the kids.

She texted back, Touch and go a couple of times, but otherwise good.

Good, Bo replied.

Ruth hesitated a moment. Maybe this wasn't a good idea, texting each other late at night, but she kept going. How about you?

I can barely get off the couch, I'm so full.

Ruth sent him a turkey emoji along with a laughing face. See you Monday.

Yup.

She appreciated that Bo had not mentioned a word about that embrace. Clearly, it wasn't as big of a deal as she'd originally thought.

Ruth thanked the Lord for helping her make it through her first Thanksgiving. "One holiday down, one big one to go. Help me through that one, too, would You, Lord?"

She didn't think she'd make it on her own.

Chapter Eleven

Monday morning, Ruth came in early to decorate the office. She hung artificial pine garland wrapped in lights around both sides of the open window between her desk and Bo's. She had enough for the kitchen area too. She chose colored strands this year and was glad for the warmth those tiny blue, green, yellow and red lights brought to the office.

As she stepped back to admire her work, the door opened, bringing in a gust of cold air. It was Bo.

She took a deep breath and smiled. "Morning."

"Good morning." He hung up his coat and brushed snow from his hair. "It looks festive in here."

"'Tis the season." So far, they were off to a normal start. Bo headed for the kitchenette. "Coffee ready?"

"Yup, just made."

Bo lifted half of an egg carton. "These are for you, and Ethan."

"The red hen's eggs?" Ruth grinned.

"After I explained how much Ethan enjoyed holding that hen, my mom made sure I brought them with me."

"Ethan will be so excited. Thank you."

"No problem. I think your son has a real love for animals. Who knows, maybe he'll decide to become a veterinarian."

Ruth considered Bo's observation. Most kids loved animals, but now that she thought about it, Ethan's appreciation was a little stronger than average. He sought out people walking their dogs so he could request a quick scratch behind canine ears. Her eight-year-old didn't hesitate to climb the tree that hung over their yard and rescue their neighbor's cat. She'd always thought he liked a good climb, but maybe there was more to it. Maybe animals were indeed Ethan's passion.

"Hmm, yeah, perhaps." Ruth counted on her boys to take over Miller Logging and Tree Service one day. It's what Cole used to say, and what he'd wanted. But what if neither of the boys wanted it?

Her mind raced ahead to a place she'd never before considered. After their annulment, Bo might marry someone else and have kids of his own. What if they wanted in on the business?

Her belly coiled tight at the thought of him marrying someone else. They were a long way off from annulment, and as business partners, they'd discuss those options then, when the time came. Silly to worry about that now. Even sillier to feel... Was that jealousy that had pinched so hard?

"Want a cup?" Bo held up a steaming mug.

"Huh?" Ruth shook her head. "I'm going to finish hanging this garland first."

Bo nodded and headed for his desk to check his email and the daily schedule of work. They'd computerized that as well, so Ruth could know where they were and what job was being done and for approximately how long.

She rolled her shoulders and grabbed the next length of garland to hang above the cabinets in the kitchenette area. At least they were speaking normally to each other. She'd worried way too much about that embrace. Bo had only tried to comfort her, not make a move. She'd been a mess and needed to be held. He held her. End of story.

Draping the garland, Ruth tried to rally a sense of relief that they were back on normal footing, but there was a little disappointment mixed in as well. Basically, she drove herself crazy with this internal tug-of-war. She'd be lying if she didn't admit her attraction for Bo, but she wasn't ready for anything more than friendly fondness.

Ruth finished with the garland and plugged it in. She'd get in the holiday mood if it killed her. She'd act normal around Bo as well, and that wouldn't kill her at all. It was the right thing to do even if a tad deflating.

Back in her office, she switched radio stations to the one that played all Christmas music and settled in to review the latest estimate requests to the smooth crooning of Bing Crosby.

"How's your mom?" she asked after a few minutes.

"She's great. She sends her best, along with a plate of cinnamon rolls, but I left them in the truck. Too worried about getting those eggs inside." He rose to fetch the goodies.

"You can get them later."

He grinned at her. "No way. I have to have one with coffee right now. They're the best."

She shook her head as Bo darted outside without his coat.

He was back in no time, with a bang of the door and another blast of cold and snow. He brushed off the snowflakes from his arms and shoulders. "It's really coming down out there."

"This is your first winter up here in how long?" Ruth asked.

"Since I was a kid. So yeah, it's been a while." He offered her a roll.

"I hope you remember how to drive in it." Ruth chuckled as she took one of the icing-laden spirals and went in for a quick bite. Her eyes may have rolled back; she couldn't be sure. "Oh. Wow. These *are* the best. Thank your mom for me."

"I will." The grin again. "And I know how to drive—" Bo's teasing stopped when the office door opened.

"Morning, Frank," Ruth said. "Bo brought cinnamon rolls."

Bo shot her an irritated glance. Evidently, he didn't want to share.

She merely grinned at him. He shouldn't have brought them inside if he wasn't prepared to share baked goods. That was a Miller Logging rule. Only private lunch pails were off-limits.

"Who made these?" Their foreman was on the treats before he'd even removed his coat.

"Bo's mom."

"Help yourself." Bo sort of shook his head. "I'll get the schedule for the day."

Ruth licked icing off her thumb as she peered toward the kitchenette. Frank grabbed coffee while Bo went over the clear-cutting job they'd put off until after Thanksgiving. It would take them the better part of a week in this weather, but the landowner wanted it done by year's end. Stretching her feet toward her little space heater as she hummed along to the tune of "Jingle Bells," Ruth didn't envy them one bit.

Bo had done his best to keep a safe distance from Ruth all week. He'd kept their conversations light and sometimes teasing, focused mainly on work. Nothing too personal. Until now. He parked his truck and stared at Ruth's Christmas card–perfect church, with real balsam wreaths on each of the big white double doors.

Owen had invited him to their Christmas program the other day, and Bo couldn't bring himself to refuse. The kid was playing a donkey in the manger, and Bo wouldn't miss it for the world. That's why he was here instead of his own church service.

Climbing up the steps, he figured he'd duck in and keep to the back pew. But once he entered the foyer, his plans of lying low crumbled when Nora spotted him.

"Bo! How nice of you to come. The boys will be thrilled." She looped her arm through his. "Here, we have plenty of room in our pew."

"Thanks." He went with her. What else could he do? Making a fuss to sit by himself would be nothing short of rude.

Ruth's eyes widened when she saw him. She stood in the middle aisle, talking with two women. One looked a little older and the other a little younger.

He nodded and took a seat next to Nora.

Ruth kept talking, but the other two women peeked over at him with curious interest.

Another reason why he shouldn't have come. He didn't want to stir any speculation with his presence. He didn't want to call attention to his growing friendship with Ruth. Apparently, she felt the same way, as his attendance to her church might as well be like any other day at the office. No big deal. Other than a sharp nip to his ego.

Looking around, he noticed that several people wore jeans. This congregation seemed far more casual than where he attended.

He hadn't needed to put on khakis and a sweater. He'd even stopped in to a local barber for a haircut the day before.

He spotted a large artificial Christmas tree, loaded with lights and bows, that took up the right corner of the altar. Battery-operated candles were perched in each window. The fake flickering light was barely visible against the gray daylight, but those candles reminded him of the walk he'd shared with Ruth and her boys at his mother's church.

With Christmas only a couple of weeks away, Bo looked forward to a holiday program, no matter how cheesy. He'd always enjoyed Christmas, but sitting here next to Nora screamed how alone he was among so many families and couples.

A middle-aged man stopped by the pew and introduced himself as the pastor. "Glad to have you."

"Bo Harris, and it's nice to be here. Thank you."

"Bo's my second cousin," Nora informed him.

"Wonderful to have family close by during the holidays. Excuse me." The pastor was tugged away by a frazzled-looking woman.

"She's the worship leader and director of the Christmas play."

Bo nodded, grateful that Nora considered him family even though he was a distant relative. He suddenly realized someone was missing. "Where's Ethan?"

Nora smiled. "Backstage."

"He's in it too?"

"He's a shepherd."

Bo wondered why Ethan hadn't mentioned anything. Both boys had been on their way to Ruth's minivan, ready to go to school, when Bo had bounded down from his apartment, running a little late. Owen had asked him to come to his Christmas play, and a pink-cheeked Ruth had filled in the time and place. Ethan hadn't said a word.

Ethan might not want him here, sitting where

Cole should be. Torn between the desire to leave and save Ethan any grief or stay put and make Owen's day kept Bo frozen in place. Which boy would be more hurt?

"Hey." Ruth slid into the pew next to him.

Great. Her soft scent teased him to inch closer. Bo rubbed the back of his neck. "Hey."

"Thanks for coming. Nice haircut, by the way."

"Not shaggy?"

Ruth chuckled. "No."

Rather than tease her some more, Bo asked, "Do you think Ethan will mind my being here?"

Ruth's hesitation spoke volumes. Ethan didn't want him here. That much was plain. "I could go."

"No." She touched his knee, then quickly drew her hand back. "Please don't. This is their first Christmas without their dad, and Ethan's taking it hard."

Bo's gut twisted. "I'm sorry."

"It's not your fault."

Twisting even tighter inside, Bo knew he needed to come clean and tell her that it might very well be his fault. But when, and how?

"Plus, I think he's a little embarrassed to be in it," Ruth explained.

"Why's that, do you think?"

Ruth shrugged. "I have no idea. All I know

is that Ethan had to be coaxed big-time to participate."

The pastor took to the stage and welcomed everyone to stand and sing before the production got underway. An older woman on the piano pounded out the Christmas hymn "O Come, All Ye Faithful."

Bo simply listened to Ruth's husky voice as she sang. With a good piano player and satin red dress, she'd beat any of the dinner-club singers he'd heard.

He finally joined in but had to bend down for a hymnal when they switched gears to "Hark! The Herald Angels Sing." He was used to words on a screen, but evidently that screen lay behind the dark velvet curtain. Leafing through the pages, he felt Ruth's hand on his arm, stilling him.

"We'll only sing the first two stanzas."

"Okay." He set the book back down and jammed his hands in his pockets to keep from touching her.

Holding her that one time had uncorked a bottleful of dangerous feelings for her. Once unleashed, he couldn't seem to wrestle them back into oblivion. She was right, though. Once they sang that last line of "glory to the newborn king," the curtains opened, revealing a shepherds-in-the-field scene.

Despite his hyperawareness of every move

Ruth made, he couldn't help but smile as he sat down along with the rest of the congregation. Ethan stood on stage, dressed as a shepherd. In one hand, he held a rounded hook, and in the other was a leash attached to a small and very real goat. The goat bleated as if on cue, and everyone laughed.

Bo glanced at Ruth, who was beaming with pride, her smile wide. With her thick red hair falling in lush waves around her shoulders, he'd never seen her look more beautiful.

She caught him staring and whispered, "What?"

"Nothing." Big fat lie, that.

Her cheeks looked a little rosier, but with the dim lighting, he couldn't be sure.

Focusing on the program, Bo enjoyed the next hour immensely. Ruth's church did a nice job performing the story of the nativity with adults and kids and some live animals. The best part for Bo was seeing Ethan shepherd not only the live goat but also Owen dressed as a donkey. They circled around the two adults portraying Joseph and Mary in the manger scene like a couple of little pros.

When the play concluded, he rose to his feet, applauding with vigor like the rest of the audience. He even spied Nora wiping away a tear.

"Oh, that was great." Nora sniffed.

"It really was." He didn't know whether to

stay or leave, so he chose the latter. "I'm going to take off."

Nora smiled. "I'm glad you came."

"Me too." Bo stepped out of the row, and bam! A small boy was clinging to his leg. Owen.

"Did you see?"

Bo chuckled. "I saw, I saw. You were a good donkey."

Owen, still wearing the costume, grinned up at him, stealing Bo's heart.

The frazzled lady came and grabbed Owen by the hand. "Time to surrender your costume, young man."

And time for Bo to leave. Turning, he nearly knocked over the dark-haired woman he'd seen Ruth talking to earlier. "I beg your pardon."

"No problem. You must be Bo Harris. I'm Erica, a friend of Ruth's."

Bo shook her outstretched hand. "Nice meeting you."

"How's business? I know Ruth was concerned."

A safe question, he supposed. "We're doing okay. New business is coming in, but I'm no Cole Miller."

Erica's wise eyes narrowed. "No one expects you to be."

Thinking of how many customers made sure he knew how much his dead boss was missed,

Bo might have to disagree. But he didn't. "No, I suppose not."

Erica gave him a warm smile. "Ruth, least of all."

Before he could ask what she meant, Erica was already moving on to someone else. But she turned slightly. "Nice meeting you. Merry Christmas."

"Yeah, Merry Christmas."

Bo had the distinct feeling that Erica knew everything. If so, Ruth hadn't abided by their marriage deal of nondisclosure. Very interesting.

Backstage, Ruth tugged on her son's coat in an attempt to get him away from the animals before she had a sneezing fit. A huge dog, a sheep and then that adorable little goat. "Come on, Ethan. Let's go."

Her son gave the goat a final pet. "Can we get one?"

Ruth laughed. "Honey, we'd need land to raise goats. They have to come in pairs, at least."

"What about the backyard?"

"That's not nearly enough room." Ruth couldn't even begin to imagine what it would take to raise goats, but she knew the puny in-town backyard they had wouldn't cut it. She ruffled her son's hair. "Come on. Owen and your grandmother are waiting for us."

"Is *he* still here?"

Ruth knew exactly who Ethan meant. "I don't know. Why does it bother you that Mr. Harris came to the play?"

Ethan shrugged.

Ruth knelt down, stopping him. Tipping up Ethan's chin so she could look him in the eye, she tried again. "Tell me."

"He's not Dad."

"Of course he's not. He's not trying to be."

Ethan's golden brown eyes shot fire. "Then why's he doing stuff for us like Dad did? Why's he so nice?"

Ruth's heart broke. Poor Ethan. He thought by liking Bo, he betrayed his father's memory. Funny how she battled those same issues.

"Ethan, Bo worked with your dad, and he's trying to help us with Dad's business. It's okay if you like him. Dad won't mind."

"How do you know?"

"Because I know your dad. You do too."

He thought that over but still looked torn.

"It's going to be okay, Ethan." Ruth gave him a quick squeeze. "Come on. Let's go home."

She really should listen to her own advice. Cole wouldn't expect her not to remarry, but four months was an awfully short time to start caring for another man. Wasn't it?

When they entered the sanctuary, Bo was gone. Having guessed that Ethan didn't want him there, it was no surprise that Bo didn't hang around. She couldn't blame him for leaving.

Deep down, Ruth hadn't wanted Bo to come to church either. Selfishly, she hadn't wanted to deal with the looks or questions about him. Other than Erica and Maddie, there were no curious stares, nor anything out of the ordinary. Shame on her for letting her five-year-old be the one to reach out and invite Bo to their Christmas play.

"Everything okay?" Nora asked.

"As good as can be expected." Ruth wrapped her arm around her mother-in-law. "Are you okay?"

Nora's brow furrowed. "I'm not going to lie—this will be a difficult Christmas without Cole and with Cash deployed."

Ruth squeezed her a little tighter, then looped her arm through Nora's. She didn't want her mother-in-law to slip on the steps. "I'm sorry. We have each other, though."

Nora patted her hand. "We do."

They headed outside into a wintry mix of sleet and freezing rain. The cleared sidewalk was now slick with a coating of ice. Ruth would take special care driving the short distance home.

The boys dashed ahead, trying to slide. They stumbled, laughed and tried again.

"Time is a good healer," Nora said.

How much time?

If anyone understood her loss, it was Nora. Her mother-in-law had lost her husband when Cole was just a teenager. She'd lost Cole, and now her youngest was in harm's way. "How do you get up every morning with a smile?"

Nora chuckled. "It's not easy, but God sustains me. Despite my loss, I have much to be thankful for. Watching your boys grow helps."

Ruth knew those words were not lightly said. She admired her mother-in-law's strong faith and always had.

"Someone cleared off your windshield and scraped the windows too." Nora elbowed her. "Bo."

Probably.

"Maybe you should invite him over for dinner. We have all that roast."

"I don't think that would be a good idea." Ruth jerked her head toward Ethan's side of the back seat.

She didn't want to push Bo on her son. She wanted their relationship to develop naturally without Ethan feeling pressured or torn between loyalties. Ruth wanted her eight-year-old to know that she had his back, now and always.

"Oh." Nora nodded.

With the boys clamoring into their seats, now was not the time to discuss the reason in detail. Ruth adjusted her mirrors and blasted the defrost setting on her heater before pulling out of the church parking lot.

By the time they got home, the tantalizing smell of pot roast filled the air, and Ruth's stomach rumbled in response.

"When do we eat?" Ethan stuffed his hat and mittens into the little shelf above the hook for his coat.

"Soon. I have to make the potatoes." Ruth picked up Owen's coat that he'd thrown on the floor.

Her youngest ran into the family room, followed by Ethan.

Ruth hung up her own coat, then headed for the kitchen to get dinner ready.

Nora remained to help. "So, what's going on with Ethan?"

Ruth made sure the boys were not within earshot. The two of them were busy in the family room, playing with the extensive LEGO set that she and Cole had given them for Christmas last year. "I think Ethan feels guilty for liking Bo."

Nora frowned. "Oh, Ruth, that's a tough one."

"It is." Ruth peeled potatoes while Nora put a pot of water to heat on the stove. "Can I ask you something?"

"Of course, dear."

Ruth had always wondered but never asked. Cole hadn't given her a good answer either. Setting down the potato she'd been holding, Ruth faced her mother-in-law. "Why didn't you re-marry?"

She smiled. "I was busy keeping Cole and Cash in line back then. And they were rambunctious. Especially Cash. I didn't have time to date—but even after the boys were out on their own, I never met the right man."

Ruth nodded and went back to peeling.

Nora laid her hand on Ruth's arm. "What I'm trying to say is that God never brought the right man my way. It's not that I didn't want to meet someone. I went on dates but didn't connect with any of them. I am grateful, though, because I've had such wonderful years here with you and Cole."

Ruth felt her throat tighten as she gripped Nora's hand. "I couldn't have dealt with his death without you."

Nora squeezed in return. "God has a plan, Ruth. He sees beyond the here and now. Place your trust in Him and His timing over your own. He knows what's best for us."

Ruth nodded.

She'd wrestled with God time and again over taking Cole from her. It didn't seem fair; but then, the Bible was full of people who'd lost their loved ones. Job had lost everything—no, God had *taken* everything from Job to test his faith. Was God testing her? Or was Cole's death simply an accident that happened because they lived in a fallen world?

Ruth read her Bible daily, but did she really heed the passages? Did she fully place her trust in the Lord?

Since Cole had died, she'd clung to the book of Romans, chapter eight. If all things were supposed to work together for her good because she loved God, when would she know that it had? How long before she realized that promise?

The business and house had been saved because of Bo. Had he been sent by God? Ruth had a habit of not waiting for God's direction. Instead, she plowed ahead to complete the tasks in front of her by her own set deadlines.

Which brought her right back to Boothe Harris. Had God truly provided a way with Bo, or had Ruth accepted this marriage deal because it was the quickest way to solve her problems?

Ruth cut the potatoes with a vengeance before sliding them into the pot of hot water. She had some time before they boiled, so she looked at Nora. "I'm going to grab my Bible a minute."

Nora nodded and continued making a salad.

She ran upstairs to her bedroom. Grabbing her Bible, Ruth leafed through the Old Testament until she found the book of Ruth. Maybe her biblical namesake could shed some light on her current situation. It was worth a try.

Reading through the short book didn't take

long, and at the end, Ruth was even more confused. She realized that both Naomi and Ruth were proactive in their choices. And Boaz had been a hesitant hero.

He may have helped them by supplying food, but he'd needed some serious prodding to step up as their kinsman redeemer. If Naomi had not instructed Ruth to sleep at the man's feet, and if Ruth hadn't acted so boldly, would Boaz have followed through?

Ruth closed her eyes. Bo had looked so good this morning at church, with that tidy new haircut and pale blue cashmere sweater. It was easy seeing him as the rich businessman he'd once been.

All this time, she'd fought against the pull she felt for Bo, and it hadn't done her any good. Her attraction had only grown into full-blown caring. She'd given Bo no indication of her feelings, nor any invitation to be more than business partners.

Other than the electricity in that one embrace, Bo hadn't exactly waved her in for more either. What if he was waiting for her to make the first move?

Something to think about and, more importantly, pray about. Ruth wasn't ready to make that first move. Not yet; but eventually, she might be. It might be sooner rather than later.

Chapter Twelve

Christmas morning came and went amid a flurry of torn wrapping paper and discarded boxes. Ruth had done her best with gifts this year. Along with the usual clothing and socks, she'd chosen a couple of fun toys for the boys. Ethan and Owen had been appreciative, but their usual excitement had been restrained. They missed their dad. Ruth did too.

While the boys played in the family room with their new squishy-darts game and the Christmas ham roasted in the oven, Ruth lounged in the living room. Lingering over another cup of a Christmas blend coffee, she stared at her artificial tree and the one wrapped gift that remained underneath.

She'd purchased a sweater for Bo and was having second thoughts about giving it to him. She'd picked out a simple dark gray wool cable-knit. The boys and Nora had signed the card as well, so she couldn't chicken out of giving it to him. But that box wrapped in red plaid mocked her for choosing such a personal gift instead of something neutral and safe for his office desk, like a coffee mug.

Buying a sweater for a man was something a girlfriend did. Or a wife...

Her phone rang, startling her. Seeing Bo's name on her screen rattled her even more. "Hello?"

"Hey, Ruth. I have a gift for Ethan and Owen, but I need your permission to give it to them. Would you mind coming up to the apartment?"

His voice sounded so chipper and friendly, as if he was talking to a buddy. Ugh!

Her hand smoothed her pulled-back hair. She hadn't heard his truck in the driveway. "You're home?"

"Yeah, got back a little while ago."

She glanced at the clock. It was only two in the afternoon. "Sure. I'll be right over."

She'd showered but that was it. No makeup. She wasn't exactly dressed for company in her leggings and long flannel shirt that used to be Cole's. Still, she didn't want to keep Bo waiting with whatever it was that he'd brought the boys.

She spotted Nora in the kitchen making tea. "I've got to run over to the apartment for a minute." Then she whispered, "Bo has a gift for the boys."

"Invite him for dinner. We have plenty."

"Yeah, that might be a good idea." Ruth wasn't sure if Bo would accept, but she'd ask.

After slipping into her boots, she headed out the door. Snow fell lightly from the sky, but it wasn't that cold. A good day to play outside, and yet she and the boys had holed up inside all morning.

Climbing up the steps to the garage apartment, Ruth tamped down the annoying mix of eagerness and nerves that jumbled through her. Bo had been at his mom's the last couple of days, so Ruth hadn't expected to see him until Monday morning at work.

Seeing him now had definitely pushed up her pulse rate. Breathing deep, she brought her hand up to knock when the door opened.

"Hurry, hurry. Come in." Bo stepped back.

Ruth dashed inside, curious. She shut the door behind her and heard a bark.

The cutest little puppy with fluffy black-and-white fur raced toward her, stumbling over Bo's boots on the way.

Ruth laughed. "You got a dog?"

"No. I brought your boys a dog."

She gave him a sharp look. "Wait, what?"

Bo scooped up the little scamp. "This is Bruno. He's a schnauzer-poodle mix, so he's supposed to be hypoallergenic. He's already house-trained and smart as a whip even though he's a little clumsy. He's fixed, has all his shots, and he's nine months old."

Ruth scratched under the dog's chin. He licked her hand, and her heart melted. "Where did you get him?"

"A friend of my mother's couldn't keep him. He's a little energetic for her. Bruno was on his way to the pound and, well, I couldn't let that happen."

"No, of course not." Ruth reached out both hands. "Can I hold him?"

"Of course. Watch out, though. He likes to chew on earlobes."

Ruth cuddled the little guy close. He didn't weigh much, so her boys could easily lift him. Rubbing her nose into his silky-soft fur, she waited for the sneeze, but nothing happened. Not even a twitch of dander tickled her senses.

"See?" Bo grinned.

Sure enough, hypoallergenic. The pup licked her ear, then latched on to one of her small wire-hoop earrings.

"No, no, Bruno." She held Bruno at arm's length and looked him over.

His eyes were dark, framed by white eyebrows. His muzzle was fuzzy, with white-and-black fur that made him look like he had a little mustache. He was the cutest thing she'd ever seen. Bruno started to squirm, so she drew him close again. "Easy, sweetie."

Bruno licked her chin.

Her boys had always wanted a dog. After losing their dad, how could she possibly refuse this time?

"Well?"

Ruth looked up into Bo's icy gray eyes, which were filled with mirth, as she handed back the dog. "Yes. You can give Bruno to the boys."

Bo smiled. "Great. I have a few things that go with him that I have to gather up, and I'll be right over."

"Anything I can help carry?"

"No. I got this."

She smiled. He wanted the boys to know Bruno came from him. And Ruth wanted that too. "I'll see you in a few." Ruth stopped at the door and turned. "Bo?"

"Yeah?"

"Were you able to have Christmas dinner?"

"My mom makes a big breakfast."

So that was a negative. He'd skipped out on Christmas dinner to bring her boys a puppy. Ruth clenched and unclenched her fists as she looked at him, deciding, wondering.

He wore a flannel shirt over a long-sleeved T-shirt, too, but unlike her red-and-black check, his was a blue-and-gray plaid that matched his eyes. Eyes that waited for her.

"Would you like to have dinner with us? It won't be ready for a little while yet."

His expression softened. "I'd love to stay for dinner."

"Great." Ruth headed out the door, down the steps and into her house before she overanalyzed the gratitude she'd read in Bo's gaze.

Maybe it was as simple as he was hungry, but she didn't think Bo wanted to spend the rest of his Christmas alone. She didn't want him to. She wanted him to spend it with them.

Finding the boys in the family room watching a kids' show, Ruth clicked off the TV to get their attention. "Bo has a gift for you, and he's coming over with it."

Owen bounced up and down, yelling, "Yay!"

"What is it?" Ethan looked much too guarded for an eight-year-old.

"I'm not telling." Ruth smiled. "Owen, hush. Plus, I invited him to have dinner with us."

"Can he sit by me?" Owen asked.

Ruth gently pinched his five-year-old nose. "I don't see why not."

"Mom…"

Ruth looked at her oldest son. "It's Christmas, Ethan."

"But—"

"Hello?" Bo's voice cut off whatever Ethan's concerns might be.

They heard an excited bark, and Ethan's eyes

grew round as saucers. He glanced at her with the most heartbreaking expression of hope.

"We're in here." Ruth couldn't stop smiling.

Nora led the way, also wearing a big smile.

Bo entered the family room with the puppy in one arm and a bag of dog stuff in the other. "Merry Christmas, Ethan and Owen. This is Bruno."

Ruth watched as her boys both fell to the floor when Bo set Bruno down. The puppy ran straight to Ethan, who scooped up the squirming bundle of black-and-white fluff and loved on him.

"For real?" Ethan's voice broke.

Ruth nodded.

Ethan kissed the puppy and set him down so Owen could pet him. Then her oldest did the most wonderful thing. He jumped to his feet, ran toward Bo and wrapped his arms around the man's waist. "Thank you."

"You're welcome, buddy." Bo patted her son's back, his voice thick.

Tears stung her eyes as she watched them. When Ethan stepped back, Bo pulled out the dog food, toys, leash and harness, and a couple of doggie sweaters for her son to inspect.

Ethan looked at her and smiled.

Ruth's heart was full. This would definitely be a Christmas to remember. A first without their dad, but also one with the sweet promise of good things ahead.

* * *

"More pie?" Ruth gathered up his plate.

"No." Bo patted his stomach and groaned. "Thanks. It was delicious, but I'm stuffed."

She smiled at him. "I'll get us more coffee."

"Sounds good." Bo stretched out his legs, tucking one ankle under the other.

It was dark outside, and the living room was dimly lit by only one lamp and the glow of the white Christmas tree lights. And a crackling fire. He could barely hear Nora talking on the phone with her other son in the family room. Ruth tinkered in the kitchen.

He leaned his head back and closed his eyes. He could get used to this—a home-cooked meal complete with pumpkin pie.

"You can stretch out if you want to nap," Ruth said softly.

He opened his eyes to the beautiful woman bringing him fragrant coffee. Yup, he could get used to this real quick.

He took the cup Ruth offered. "It doesn't get much better than this, does it?"

She set her mug on the coffee table and sat right next to him. A bittersweet expression took over her face, as if she remembered many happy Christmases before. "Sometimes."

"Sorry. Poor choice of words." He could have kicked himself. This was her first Christmas without Cole. It was far from good for her.

"It's okay." Ruth poked his side with her elbow. "I'm glad you're comfortable here."

"Me too." Maybe too comfortable, all things considered.

She leaned forward as if to get up. "Oh no, we forgot to give you our gift."

"Later." He touched her shoulder. He didn't want her moving away from him to another chair.

She grabbed her steaming mug and leaned back.

When her shoulder touched his arm, he draped it across the back of the couch. His fingertips brushed her other shoulder. He held his breath, feeling like a teen hoping she wouldn't scoot away. She didn't.

He wanted to prolong the peaceful quiet that permeated the room, so he didn't make any grand gestures. He simply soaked in the sensation of Ruth sitting close. The boys were asleep on the floor near the tree, and Bruno lay right between them, zonked. And no wonder. Bo and the boys had played outside in the snow with Bruno. The little pup had worn a sweater and didn't seem to mind the cold as he chased snowballs.

"Thank you for the puppy. The boys love him." Ruth's voice was low. Soft.

"You're welcome." Bo took another sip, keeping his voice quiet as well. "I have more good news. I talked to my friend Rick, and it looks like the forest supervisor welcomes our bid for consideration. We'll have to work on it this week so we're ready come January."

Ruth looked up at him. "That is good news." Then she scrunched her nose. "Do we know how?"

Bo chuckled. He was well versed in making bids and pitches to either acquire or sell businesses. "We'll figure it out with Frank's help."

"Yeah. We'll figure it out." Ruth leaned a little closer, letting her head rest against his shoulder.

There was more to figure out when it came to the two of them. He didn't want to rush anything, but his feelings were in a tangle when it came to Ruth. He was falling in love with her, but telling her that might well ruin this moment.

Memorizing the feel of her against him and the citrusy scent of her hair, Bo simply enjoyed it and tried to keep condemning thoughts at bay. Even if he had the guts to say something, his conscience wouldn't let him profess any feelings before he'd confessed to his part in Cole's death.

Christmas Day was not the time to do either.

Bo set down his coffee cup before he dropped it.

"Do you want me to move over?" Ruth whispered.

"No." He gave her shoulder a squeeze.

"Merry Christmas, Bo."

He rested his cheek against the top of her head. "Merry Christmas, Ruth."

"Mom?" Ethan sat up, awake.

Ruth leaned forward. "Yes, Ethan."

His side felt cold where she used to be.

"Mr. Harris didn't open his gift." The boy reached for the box.

At least the kid didn't eye him with suspicion anymore. But then, Ethan hadn't seen him with his arm around Ruth. Tricky stuff, this marriage deal. Bo wanted to make it real, but he'd need the kids' buy-in and Nora's too—although he had a feeling Ruth's mother-in-law already approved.

His stomach soured. All that could change once he told Ruth what happened the day Cole died. Nora would surely hold it against him, and he'd lose all this. This feeling of family.

Letting loose a sigh, Bo smiled at Ethan. "I think we better take Bruno outside first."

The puppy yawned, then wagged his tail.

"I'll take him." Ethan headed for the side door to the backyard.

Ruth turned to him. "You said he rings a bell when he has to go out?"

"Yeah, Mom's friend had trained him that way. It's a jingle bell at the end of a length of ribbon. Just hang it on the door you want Bruno to head for when he's got to go."

"That's a good idea."

"What is?" Owen was awake too.

Ruth chuckled. "I'll show you later." She stood and reached for Bo's coffee cup. "There goes the quiet evening."

"I should probably head back to the apartment anyway." He stretched his arms behind his head before he pulled her back down next to him.

Ethan returned, with Bruno bouncing at his heels.

Nora stepped in right behind them.

"We're all here," Ruth said. "Owen, will you give Mr. Harris his gift?"

Owen handed Bo the wrapped present. "Mom bought it."

Bo glanced at Ruth, and her cheeks were pink. He opened the Christmas card, signed by all, and then moved on to ripping open the box. It made the boys laugh.

After pulling out a nice wool sweater the color of slate, he looked at Ruth, feeling like a heel. He should have gotten her something. "Thank you."

She shrugged. "I wasn't sure but saw it on sale—"

"It's great. Thank you." He stood. "And I should head out. Thanks for dinner."

Ethan stood as well, smiling. "Thanks for Bruno, Mr. Harris."

"You're welcome." He smiled back at the boy, then the rest of them. He'd have to talk to Ruth about her boys calling him plain old Bo from now on. "Good night."

"I'll walk you out," Ruth said.

Bo stalled her. "Stay and enjoy your family."

She smiled. "Okay."

He made his escape. The last thing he needed was Ruth on the doorstep, bidding him goodnight. He'd kiss her for sure. Tonight wasn't the right time, and her laundry room stoop definitely wasn't the place.

Ruth listened as Bo and Frank went over typical charges for selective hardwood cuttings, both with and without keeping the wood. Since Bo was jotting down the figures, she mentally checked out when they started listing expenses once again.

How long would it take to crunch those numbers? Ruth had no idea about the numbers. She had to trust Bo and Frank. They had kept repeating the obvious—if they bid too high, they might lose the contract; bid too low and they'd lose profits.

"Water, anyone?" Ruth asked.

Bo shook his head, and Frank declined as well.

It was late in the afternoon, the day nearly done. They'd only needed one crew this week since there were not many jobs scheduled between Christmas and New Year's. With the exception of Bo and Frank, the rest of the staff had agreed to work either the start of the week or the end so that everyone could enjoy a little holiday time off. Including her. She was only in today.

Ruth got up for a bottle of water. Instead of sitting back down, she leaned against the kitchen counter and watched Bo. He wore the sweater she'd bought him, and he looked pretty good in it too. He was a good man. Giving the boys a dog that didn't make her sneeze and snow-blowing the driveway on Sunday so they could get out to work today were both proof of that fact.

In the three and a half months since they'd entered this marriage deal, Bo had exceeded her expectations. He wasn't merely a business partner, and he'd gone beyond a simple tenant as well. He made sure the woodbin stayed full. He'd painted the fence, raked the leaves and now took care of snow-blowing the driveway.

She would never have sold Cole's truck if Bo hadn't found the buyer while he was out on a job. He'd become a true friend and more. Did she want more? Yes, maybe she did. Life partner? It was too soon yet to make that call.

Ruth couldn't shake how relaxing it had been leaning against Bo on Christmas Day. Safe, even, with no pressure or demands. She could have cuddled up with him on that couch and watched the tree lights all night.

They'd turned a corner with Ethan as well.

Bruno had done that. Her son seemed to have accepted Bo. Or maybe, her son had finally come to terms with liking the man. Ruth had as well. She liked Bo. A lot.

Bo glanced her way. "I think we can get started on putting a bid together."

Frank looked at his watch. "Quitting time."

Bo looked surprised. "I guess it is. Have a good night, Frank. I'll see what I can come up with and have you look at it tomorrow."

"Sounds good."

"See you next year, Frank." Ruth waved.

After he left, she approached Bo. "Anything I can do?"

"It's getting late. We can pick up tomorrow."

Ruth shook her head. "I'm off the rest of the week, remember? The kids are home, and I can't expect Nora to watch them all week."

Bo nodded. "That's right."

"But I can stay late tonight. Let me call and see if she'll take care of dinner." Ruth dialed her mother-in-law and got the clearance to stay as long as needed. "All set."

"All right, let's head to your office. You're good at adding the sparkle."

Ruth laughed. "The what?"

"The marketing slant, the PR pizzazz, whatever you want to call it. You have a good eye for making what we do look attractive."

The compliment warmed her all the way down to her toes. "Then let's make some sparkle."

"Let's." Bo's eyes looked darker than normal. Maybe it was the slate color of the sweater that made his stare so magnetic. Or maybe it was the way he was looking at her that drew her in. Whatever it was, her gaze was locked into his for at least a second or two before he stepped back to let her pass into her office.

"After you."

"Thanks." Ruth sat at her desk and scooted over, making room for Bo and his list of numbers. She needed to focus on the task at hand and quit mooning over him. "How should I structure this?"

He pulled a chair around. Pointing to the screen, he said, "Start with this number in bold. Then we will list what we bring for that figure."

Ruth stared at the large dollar amount. It seemed huge to her. "Are you sure about this?"

"As sure as I've ever been about anything."

"Okay." Ruth blew out her breath.

If only some of his confidence would rub off on her. Requesting payment for an amount that large sure seemed like business suicide.

Chapter Thirteen

After ninety minutes, Bo leaned back in the chair and rubbed his eyes. "I think we have a good rough draft."

Ruth pulled a flash drive out of her desk drawer and stuck it in her computer. "I can tinker with it this week while I'm home."

"That'd be great." He could touch base with her some evening and see if she needed any help. It'd be a good excuse to see her.

He glanced out the window at the snow falling. Heavy lake-effect bands were predicted overnight, so they had some time before the heavy stuff fell. "Want to get something to eat?"

Ruth checked her watch. "Dinner's over at home, so yeah, that'd work."

"Any preference where to go?" Bo slipped into his coat and grabbed hers from the rack by the door.

Ruth shrugged. "The diner is fine."

"Diner it is. Come on. I'll drive." Bo held Ruth's coat open for her.

She pulled a cream-colored knitted hat and scarf out of one sleeve and put them on. Slipping into her long, puffy red coat, she looked up at him. Pretty and fresh-faced, she belonged in a Christmas card commercial. "Thank you."

"Welcome." He smiled back.

They left the office, climbed into his truck and headed into town. The snow had picked up a little by the time they pulled into the diner where they'd first met.

The windows were glazed over with canned snow and outlined with the big old-fashioned colored Christmas lights. Their electric bill must take a hit this time of year. Bo held the door for Ruth, and the comforting aroma of fried food wrapped around him like a security blanket.

Once seated, Bo didn't bother with the menu.

Ruth peeked above hers. "Do you know what you want?"

"The Monday-night special is a meat loaf dinner, complete with real mashed potatoes. It's pretty good too."

She smiled. "I take it you've had it before."

"Nearly every Monday. I swing by here on my way home."

A frown marred the perfect skin of her forehead.

"What?"

She shrugged. "Maybe you should eat dinner with us a little more."

"Maybe you should invite me."

She laughed. "Touché."

Her laugh was a rich sound he never tired of hearing. It sure seemed like she laughed more these days. Was that a sign of healing? He hoped so.

A waitress delivered glasses of water and then took their orders. *Ruth and her salads...* She'd ordered the chef variety.

"How's Bruno?" Bo took a long drink.

"Wonderful. He's a good puppy, but he likes to chew up socks. I have to keep them at the bottom of the laundry basket, or he'll find them."

"I saw Ethan take him out this morning." Bo recalled the cute vision of a sleepy eight-year-old in his pajamas and boots, waiting for the puppy to do his business.

"He's serious about taking care of Bruno. He feeds him, makes sure he's got clean water and jumps to take him out every time the bell rings. It's pretty neat, but it's still all new. Ethan might eventually slack off when it becomes a chore."

"He might enjoy the responsibility. Ethan's a good worker. He didn't give up on painting the fence and stuck with me to the end."

"Yeah, he's a pretty good kid, if I do say so." Ruth smiled. "What about you? Did you grow up taking care of more than a dog and sheep?"

Bo nodded. "My grandfather raised the sheep, but we did have a cow."

"Really? Just one?"

"Yup. My grandmother liked fresh milk. I remember her saying in broken English that no self-respecting Finn drank their milk from a carton. She was pretty old-fashioned."

Ruth's eyes widened. "Is there a big difference?"

"Raw milk is thicker, richer. Grandma used to leave in some of the cream. She made butter too. The best I've ever tasted. Funny, but I was embarrassed by those rural roots when I was a teenager at private school. Little things seemed like such a big deal back then."

"I know. My sister and I used to hate wearing our winter boots because they were so clunky, but they were warm."

Bo chuckled. He could easily imagine her as a sassy teen, giving her mother grief about clunky boots.

Their food arrived, and Bo couldn't help but notice the difference a few months had made between them. The last time they'd gone to dinner together was the day they'd married. It had been such an awkward outing, and now they chatted easily. Comfortably.

Ruth looked up at him. "Something wrong with your food?"

He hadn't touched his meat loaf yet. "I was

just thinking about the last time we went to dinner, in Marquette."

"Seems like a lifetime ago." Ruth's golden eyes turned sad.

"Not that long." Bo was sorry to have dampened the mood. "At least we're more comfortable now."

"Yeah." Ruth didn't look too comfortable with this conversation.

They'd become friends. Lots of people did when they worked together. The fact that she'd given him a Christmas gift and sat close to him that evening didn't mean she had any stronger feelings for him.

"So, tell me the process for submitting a bid," Ruth said.

This was safe ground, so Bo obliged. "Some time after the first of the year, I'll get a call or email from the forest supervisor with instructions to submit a bid. Then, if he likes what we've provided, he'll set up a meeting. Hopefully, we'll land the contract."

Ruth covered his hand with hers. "Thank you for seeing this through—for taking the business where Cole wanted it to go."

Bo gripped her hand and squeezed. "It's a good direction."

"I think so too." She stared at their joined hands for a moment before pulling hers back.

Bo finished his meal, running over their timeline. Five months since her husband's death was still too soon to expect anything more than friendship between them. He'd simply bide his time. But before too long, he had to tell her the truth.

Ruth pulled the collar of her coat tighter as they walked outside to Bo's truck. The wind had picked up, and the snow was thick and falling fast. "Yikes."

Bo's expression was a stern one. "Yeah. I think I should just drive us home. We can get your minivan tomorrow."

"Okay." Ruth was no coward when it came to winter driving, but visibility was practically nonexistent. She had no problem leaving her car at the office. "Good thing it's Christmas break, or tomorrow might be a snow day."

Bo started the truck as she climbed in the passenger side. He brushed off the windows and windshield, having to scrape the ice that had built up while they'd been in the diner.

Ruth had already texted Nora about their dinner plans so her mother-in-law wouldn't worry. Cranking the heat, Ruth snuggled deeper into her coat and watched Bo. There was a solid strength in him that she'd never wanted to notice before.

She noticed it now and shivered.

He opened the back door and threw the snow

brush inside, then climbed in behind the wheel. "Ready?"

Was she? Maybe.

"Hey, I never thanked you for clearing off the minivan the day of the Christmas program. So thank you."

"No problem." He lowered the heat and backed out.

Driving home took longer than it should have. Ruth remained quiet as Bo concentrated on keeping his truck on the road in a full-blown whiteout. Despite the hazardous driving conditions, he seemed distant. The warmth of their dinner conversation had waned into awkward silence once again.

Ruth had to own that they didn't do too well alone unless they were at work. Glancing at his profile, which might as well be carved out of stone, she wondered if he also felt this new awareness between them. Maybe that's what troubled him. They were veering away from their keep-it-strictly-business plan.

When they pulled into the driveway, the house looked pretty dark, with the exception of the kitchen light left on. The boys might already be in bed. And that meant Nora wasn't far from turning in as well. Not a good time to ask Bo to come in.

Bo placed the truck in Park and turned off the engine. "If you want to drive in with me to get your car, text me in the morning, and I'll wait for you."

"Okay." Ruth tried to unbuckle the seat belt. It didn't unlatch. Peeling off her mittens, she tried again. Nothing.

She glanced at Bo. "It's stuck."

He unbuckled his seat belt with no problem and leaned over. He pulled a couple of times, but nothing happened.

She really was stuck.

Leaning down, he examined the belt's connection. "Here's the problem. Your scarf is clicked into the buckle." He looked up. "I might have to tear it."

Ruth caught her breath at how close his face hovered near her own. "Okay."

He yanked on the scarf. Finding no purchase, he pulled even harder, and bam! He popped her so hard under her chin, she thought her teeth rattled.

"Ow!"

"Ruth, I'm so sorry." He looked horrified. "I am so, so sorry. Let me see."

She felt his fingers probing along her jaw as she opened and then closed her mouth. "No harm done."

He held up her scarf. "It's out."

Ruth laughed. "Good thing too. I think another hit like that might be a knock-out."

He didn't find the humor in her statement.

With a deep and endearing frown, Bo zoomed in again, gently lifting her chin. "I sure hope you don't get a bruise."

She laughed. "I'll be fine."

"I hope so." His voice sounded raspy.

She looked up, caught his gaze and held it, her heart racing.

He didn't move, either, just stared at her as if considering what to do next.

The interior of the truck cab seemed to shrink in on them, like they were trapped in a shaken snow globe. The heat had long since been turned off with the truck engine, but Ruth flushed, suddenly overwarm.

She knew exactly what to do. Taking a deep breath, she ran her hand up into his surprisingly soft, short blond hair. Tipping her face up, she pulled Bo close enough for their lips to barely touch.

Ruth hesitated only for a heartbeat before leaning in.

She felt his arms wrap around her as he returned her kiss—gentle at first, then more insistent, as if he couldn't get enough. The sensation was dizzying. Her heart beat so fast that her mind went spinning into oblivion.

One kiss turned into two, then three and—

Ruth came up for air. "Wait… We can't."

"We can."

Bo's lips traveled along her jaw, down to her

neck. He hadn't shaved, and the whiskers on his chin tickled her skin. "We're married, remember?"

He might as well have poured a bucket of ice water over her head. Ruth pushed him away. "On paper, maybe, but a marriage deal is not how it's supposed to be."

Bo looked confused, then annoyed. "How's it supposed to be?"

"You know." He'd been engaged before.

And then Ruth remembered that his ex had been in it for the money. Just like her. Regret wasn't a good dish eaten on a full stomach, and Ruth was going to lose it as guilt swamped her.

She managed a rough whisper. "It's supposed to be about love."

Bo's color was high, but he didn't say a word. Not one.

Ruth waited, hoping, but he still didn't say anything.

And that hurt. Didn't he feel anything for her? Or was he thinking about his trust fund and wondering if she was going after it too?

After grabbing the seat belt buckle, which finally came loose, she got out of the truck and dashed toward the house. Without looking back, she went inside and stripped off her coat.

Stuffing her fist against her mouth to stop the sob ready to rip loose, Ruth took a deep breath instead. She had to get it together before Nora heard her. Before the boys saw her.

But the house was quiet.

Slipping into the kitchen, she glanced at the clock on the stove, and her stomach sank. It was after ten. How long had they been out there in his truck, fogging up the windows like a couple of kids?

With a shaking hand, Ruth opened the fridge and grabbed a bottle of water. She went upstairs and listened at Nora's closed bedroom door. Should she tell her what happened? Nora would have wise words, but there was only silence beyond the door.

Then she went to the boys' door, which was slightly ajar. Listening, she heard only soft breathing. She gently pushed open the door, and Bruno lifted his head. The pup lay at the foot of Ethan's twin bed.

Quietly, Ruth entered the room. Glancing at Owen's bed to make sure her youngest was still covered up, she scooped up the dog. Nuzzling him close, she slipped out of her boys' room and went downstairs.

"Come on, fella. Let's go outside." She stepped into the backyard and set down the dog.

Bruno took his time sniffing around, so Ruth looked up at the window to Bo's apartment. The lights were on, but the mini-blinds were drawn closed. What was he thinking right now? Ruth squeezed her eyes shut, then opened them wide. He'd think she was an idiot, and he'd be right. They'd had a deal, and she'd broken it. They both had.

Bruno finally did his business and quietly returned to her feet, shaking as if he just realized he was outside in the cold snow.

Ruth picked up the dog and went back inside. Still holding Bruno, she kicked off her boots. "What am I going to do, huh, fella? I really blew it."

The pup looked at her, then licked her chin.

Ruth snuggled the dog, then climbed the stairs and quietly deposited Bruno back onto Ethan's bed. The dog curled up against the curve of her son's legs with a soft groan.

It made her smile. Bruno was the sweetest of gifts.

Exiting her sons' bedroom, Ruth leaned against the wall and slid to the floor. Was she really falling for Bo or simply lonely and missing her husband?

She knew the latter was true, but she couldn't be sure about the former. Even so, shame on her for leading Bo on and then proverbially slapping his face when he'd responded. She was a horrible woman. And now Bo probably thought so too.

Ruth buried her face in her hands and let silent tears fall.

* * *

The next morning, Bo started up the snow-blower. All told, they must have gotten at least eight inches or more of accumulation overnight. The sky was lightening in the east, but the sun hadn't risen yet. He glanced at the house and spotted Ruth at the window in a fuzzy blue robe.

He gritted his teeth.

She held up her phone.

He nodded and pulled his phone out of his pocket and read her text.

We need to talk.

Didn't he know it. He'd been so close to admitting his feelings but knew it'd be a mistake to say so before telling her the truth.

He texted back, I'll clear the drive and then we can talk on the way to the office and your car.

Her response was a simple Okay.

He took his time snow-blowing. There wasn't that much to do since the driveway was short, but he went out of his way to clear a path in the backyard for the dog. A loop for the little guy to run the perimeter.

He wasn't looking forward to this conversation. Not one bit.

After putting away the snowblower, he turned and there was Ruth. Bundled in her red down coat and matching red hat with a white ball on top, she looked awfully vulnerable without makeup.

"Ready?" She swung her purse over her shoulder.

"As ready as I'll ever be." He didn't wait for her response. He climbed into the truck and started it, then waited for the engine to warm a little before turning up the heat.

Ruth had climbed in and buckled her seat belt; then she gave him a cheeky grin. "My scarf is firmly tucked into my coat this time."

His laugh sounded more like a bark.

"You okay?"

He turned toward her. "Look, I'm sorry about last night."

She shook her head. "You have nothing to apologize for. It was me. My fault, I started it."

"No, Ruth, I have everything to apologize for." His voice sounded strained even to his own ears. "I haven't been up front with you."

Her eyes widened, and she looked scared. "What do you mean?"

He took a steadying breath, but his gut was twisted in knots. He was scared too. He loved her, but there was no way he could tell her until she knew how her husband had died. When he did tell her—

"I may have caused that tree to fall the wrong way."

She tipped her head. "What tree…"

She went pale.

"I don't know if I secured the main pull rope. I don't think I did, Ruth. It's my fault Cole died." There. He'd finally said it out loud.

Confessing didn't do a thing to dull the ache in his chest. He watched her take it all in, hoping they might still have a chance; but in his gut, he knew better.

"How do you know?" Her voice cracked.

He shrugged and gazed out the truck's windshield, trying to remember that one crucial step. He couldn't. "I just know."

"Why didn't you tell me this sooner?"

That was the million-dollar question. He rubbed his face with both hands and turned to her again. "Would you have agreed to our deal if I had?"

She looked at him, white as a sheet, and then splotchy color flushed her face. Those golden eyes of hers narrowed, and if looks could kill, he'd be dead. "No, I wouldn't have."

"Ruth, listen—"

She held up her hand. "Not now."

"If not now, when?"

She looked crushed. "Please, just drive."

He wanted to argue, wanted to defend himself somehow, but what could he really say? He pulled out of the driveway, glad the road had been plowed. At least she'd make it back home safely.

Grateful their commute to the office trailer was relatively short, Bo remained quiet for the first few blocks until he couldn't stand the silence any longer. "When you called me, I knew I needed to make amends somehow."

He could see that her jaw was clenched, and she remained quiet, so he continued. "I owed it to you to save the business."

She lashed out then. "And what about you? You're falling into a sweet deal along with access to your trust fund."

He spotted Frank with his plow truck, clearing the lot as he pulled in. "It wasn't like that."

"Right." Her low voice dripped sarcasm.

The minivan was snow-covered, but Ruth would be able to get out with little problem. As he pulled in next to it, she was already unbuckled and opening the passenger door.

"Ruth, wait."

She slammed the door.

He blew out a breath.

That didn't go well. But then, what had he expected? He shut off his truck as she climbed into her car. He got out, snowbrush in hand. He heard the minivan start and began brushing off her windshield. He didn't want her driving out of here without clear windows.

Thankfully, she let him do it, but she wouldn't look at him. Seeing her with her head down was like a sucker punch to the stomach. He should have told her sooner. Much sooner. But the reality of his question remained: Would she really have let him help her?

He'd just finished the back window when she backed up. He quickly stepped out of the way and watched, helpless, as she pulled out onto the street, driving faster than she should.

Frank had stopped his truck and rolled down his window. "You two have a fight?"

Bo continued to watch Ruth's minivan careen down the road. "You could say that."

"Flowers get me out of trouble every time." Frank winked.

Since when did Frank look at them like a couple? He could hedge around the obvious attraction he'd had for Ruth, but what point was there? He kicked at the snow. "She'd probably throw them back in my face."

"That bad, huh?"

"Yeah." Bo headed for the office trailer.

"I'll be done in a bit." Frank returned to plowing the lot as a few of the week's early crew pulled in.

Bo could tell Frank what he'd told Ruth, but what good would it do to bring the foreman back to that day and confirm what he already knew down deep? Frank had loved Cole. Everyone had. It was one of the many things Bo had envied about the man. Cole's employees worked hard for more than just a paycheck or love of the job. They'd admired the man who'd led them.

He stepped into the office, hung up his coat and went to make coffee. It was good Ruth had the rest of the week off. He'd give her some space before trying to talk to her again. What he'd say, he had no idea.

Chapter Fourteen

Instead of driving home, Ruth headed for the cemetery. Tears streamed down her cheeks, but she furiously brushed them away. She'd been played.

Months ago, she'd felt like Bo had been orchestrating everything. She'd ignored those warning signs because she'd been desperate and pressed for time. *Stupid, stupid, stupid!*

After pulling into the small parking lot, which had been plowed, Ruth got out and looked around. The drivable path to Cole's gravesite had not yet been cleared, but that didn't matter. She wore warm winter boots and could make it on foot.

The snow was dense, but she trudged through it, working up a sweat as she went. Her breath came out in quick bursts of mist in front of her, and the cold air burned as she sucked it back in.

The bite of the morning temperatures served her right for being a fool.

Finally reaching Cole's headstone, Ruth dropped to her knees. Only his body remained in the ground—she knew that—but overwhelmed by the need to talk to her dead husband, she blurted, "What really happened that day, Cole?"

Ruth didn't expect an answer, but the silence still bothered her. It made her mad. With mitten-clad hands, she dug at the snow that covered her husband's dates of birth and death. Digging deeper, she knocked aside the jars with candles she'd placed there with Nora and the boys.

All too clearly, she remembered sharing in the Finnish traditions with Bo and his mom. The sweetness of it had been real, as well as the closure she'd found by repeating it here, at Cole's grave. She'd thought it a blessing at the time.

The memory of Bo sharing some of himself with her pricked like a thorn in her flesh. Had he been real with her at all?

Leaning back on her heels, she listened to the sounds of chickadees calling in the distance. Sunshine streamed through the bare trees, making the snowy branches glisten and sparkle. It was beautiful. It was heartbreaking.

"What do I do?" Even to her own ears, her voice sounded tangled with pain.

She didn't know which was worse: the fact that Bo had kept this information from her or the reason he'd stayed silent. Was guilt his motivation for their marriage deal or was it access to his trust fund and the business?

Closing her eyes, Ruth heard Bo's words with chilling clarity. *Would you have agreed to our deal?*

What if he hadn't secured that rope on purpose?

Ruth rejected that horrible thought. Bo was no killer. He'd professed to be a man of faith, and she wasn't about to question that just because he'd done her wrong. The Bible told stories of believing men who'd traded their integrity for greed.

Besides, she'd called Bo first. He hadn't approached her. Not even at Cole's funeral. He'd said that he'd gone, but she'd never noticed him. Had he lied about that too?

The ceremony and meal afterward had been a blur. She'd pasted on a brave face to get through it, and her face had actually hurt from so many forced smiles. There had been so many people, she couldn't remember who was there and who wasn't.

As she knelt in the snow, staring at her husband's headstone, Cole's funeral seemed like another lifetime. So many things had happened since then, like nearly losing her home.

If Bo had been after Miller Logging and Tree Service all along, he could have taken advantage of the opportunity she'd presented him. He'd known about the financial difficulties, and yet he'd wanted on board. He'd been the head of mergers and acquisitions at Harris Industries, so he had to be shrewd when it came to business. Ruthless, even. Had he been softening her up all this time so he could eventually take control of the business?

It's not as if Bo had tried to romance her into handing over control. She'd been the one to kiss him first. She'd even worried that Bo might think *she'd* been manipulating *him. Ha!*

The kisses they'd shared sure felt real—at least, she'd thought so at the time. And Nora had liked Bo from the start; what would she think now? And her boys? They'd grown to care for him too. Cole may have trusted Bo, but she couldn't. Not anymore.

Running her hand across her husband's name, Ruth made a solemn promise. "I'm going to make this right."

How to do that was beyond her at this point, but she'd find a way. She'd figure it out. Ruth stood and shivered when the wet fabric of her jeans where she'd knelt clung to her skin. The bitter cold seeped into her very bones, making her shake with deep shivers.

She had to get home.

She also needed a plan of action.

It sure seemed like she had a pattern of letting

the men she loved pull the wool over her eyes by not sharing the whole truth. First Cole, now Bo.

Ruth froze. Did she love Bo?

Tears stung her eyes. She couldn't love him. Love was built on trust, and that tender trust was gone. Whatever feelings she'd had for him had been ruined by that one sentence ringing in her ears. Over and over she kept hearing, *Would you have agreed to our deal?*

Ruth got back in the minivan and drove home. She'd agreed to marry Bo out of desperation. This time, she wanted options. Ruth was done with her desire to be taken care of. That was God's job. And hers.

If there was one thing she'd learned over the past few months, it was that she could adapt. She could do what needed done. Miller Logging and Tree Service had a very good reputation, and that had to be worth something.

She'd wanted to save Cole's business for Ethan and Owen, but with Bo at the helm, it might not be the same company when her sons were old enough to take over. If either of them even wanted it. Bo's observation of Ethan's interest in animals had been a good one. One she'd not paid close enough attention to. And Owen? Who knew what he'd want to become when he grew up.

The reality was that even though they had signed an agreement that had granted her the controlling share of the company, Ruth didn't know business like Bo Harris. She'd deferred to his judgment time and time again.

Could they really remain partners after this? Ruth didn't think so. She wasn't going to roll over and play dead until she knew. She'd find out her options and then make a decision.

After pulling into the driveway, she turned off the engine and headed for the house. With a deep breath, she forced an expression of calm on her face. It was only midmorning when she entered the family room. Nora and the boys were still in their pajamas, piecing together a puzzle that had been a gift from her parents. They were clustered around a card table.

"Hi, Mom." Ethan waved.

She bent and kissed her boy's head. "Has Bruno been outside?"

"Ethan took him out about half an hour ago." Nora snapped a puzzle piece into place, closing in the border.

"Nice job." Ruth loved puzzles, but she was in no mood to play now. "I've got some work to do. I'll be upstairs if you need me."

Nora didn't look up from the similar pieces of sky she was comparing. "I thought you were taking this week off."

"I am, but this is about that bid to the US Forest Service. I need to look over the rough draft."

"Look what I did." Owen had a swatch of

pieces crammed together that didn't belong. He'd bend those pieces if he kept it up.

Ruth kissed his cheek. "Owen, maybe you should work on your coloring books."

He shrugged off her touch. "I want to puzzle."

Nora glanced up. "He's fine. Go do what you need to do."

It was only a puzzle. Put together today and then stored away tomorrow. Did it really matter if a few pieces were bent? Probably not.

"You're the best." Ruth rubbed her mother-in-law's shoulder. Should she tell her what Bo had said? It would hurt her so deeply. Cole was her son.

"I know." Nora patted her hand.

Ruth decided not to say a word. Not now. Maybe never.

Once upstairs in her room, Ruth changed into warm leggings, wrapped a fuzzy throw around her shoulders and opened up her laptop. She pulled out the flash drive from her purse and plugged it into the side. There was financial information about Miller Logging on that bid.

Opening up the draft, she found what she needed. Grabbing a pen, notebook and her phone, she searched out Miller Logging and Tree Service's competition and then jotted down their respective numbers. She knew the estimated worth of her husband's business, but the only way to know its real value was to find out how much someone might be willing to pay for it.

Selling Cole's business outright was one option. If the price was right, she could pay off the bank and Bo's initial investment. Their business deal would become null and void. She could then seek that annulment, and they could go their separate ways.

She could go back to work in a dental office and save up for recertification as a dental hygienist. Without the pressure of that business loan hanging over her head, she could do it. Ruth could still provide for her family.

Chewing her thumbnail, she realized that plan didn't guarantee jobs for Frank and the crew. But if Ruth could make their positions a stipulation of the sale, selling might be a viable option.

Would Cole approve?

No. He wouldn't.

Ruth rubbed her cheeks and then her eyes. "I'm sorry, honey, but I have to at least find out the particulars. In the end, I might have to sell."

How would she explain why she'd sold after Bo had saved the day?

Ruth shook off the image of a very disappointed mother-in-law and grabbed her cell. Entering the first phone number into the keypad, Ruth made the call before she lost her nerve.

That night, Bo climbed the steps to the garage apartment with a heavy heart. Ruth wouldn't answer his calls. He'd finally texted her that he needed to explain, but she'd texted back that he didn't. She'd said that he'd been perfectly clear this morning.

Once inside, he took off his coat and picked up his phone. Dialing a number he didn't often call, Bo waited.

"Bo, good to hear from you, son. Thanks for the Christmas card." His father sounded tired.

"How was your holiday?" Bo sat on the couch and stretched out his legs.

"Busy. I take it there's a reason for your call." His father never bothered with small talk.

Bo followed his father's lead. "Is there leeway on the year requirement to access my trust?"

"You need cash?"

"I'd like to buy into Miller Logging early and pay off the note." Then he could turn it all over to Ruth. Maybe that would prove to her that he hadn't been as mercenary as he'd sounded.

His father chuckled. "You'll have to stick out the year of marriage. Those are the terms."

Bo fought frustration. "But you made the terms."

"And set them into a legally binding trust agreement. It's not something I can undo quickly, nor do I want to."

"Why? Why'd you ever set up that trust in the first place?"

He heard his father's sigh. "To protect you. In case you chose a different path than mine.

Which is exactly what you ended up doing when you left here."

"But why the marriage clause?"

Again, his father chuckled. "So you'd leave behind a living legacy of a family. I should have known that Sheri wasn't right for you. Perhaps this Miller woman is."

Ruth was the one he wanted, but he'd lost her.

"So that's it." Bo knew there was no moving his father's decision once made.

"You've got a year. Why don't you come down for New Year's? Bring your wife."

Was his father mocking him? He knew the marriage was an agreement, a business deal. "Thanks, but I have an important bid coming up."

"Another time." Was that disappointment he heard in his father's voice?

"Yeah. Some other time. I promise." Bo ended the call. It had been worth a try.

He wanted Ruth to know that he wasn't in this for himself. Sure, he'd seen the advantage at first, but that's not why he'd proposed buying into Miller Logging and Tree Service. And that's not why he'd kept his part in Cole's death from her. He'd sign the whole business back over to her, draw up another deal between them—but first, he had to talk to her.

Ruth clearly didn't want to talk to him.

He sat in the dark, contemplating the rest of

the week. Three more days until the work week was over. He'd give Ruth space for the next three days before—what?

He played the conversation with his father over in his mind. Ruth Miller was the right woman for him, but what if she couldn't overcome what he'd told her? Even if she did, his negligence would always stand between them. And there was Ethan and Owen to consider as well. Would Ruth want them to know about it one day?

He sucked in his breath. Nora would hate him. Cole was her son.

He didn't see a way out of this situation that ended well. He laid his head back and stared at the ceiling. Why hadn't he kept his distance? He knew from the beginning that he couldn't have Ruth, and yet he'd let her inside. He'd let himself love her.

Closing his eyes, Bo sought help from the only One who could fix this. He prayed that God would somehow make a way.

Friday afternoon, New Year's Eve, Ruth pulled into the office trailer parking lot and got out. No one was around. Bo had texted her that he and Frank had closed up shop at lunchtime. He planned to go to his mother's for the weekend. It was the first text he'd sent her in three days. She'd hated the way her heart had leaped at seeing a message from him flash across her cell's screen. Even though she'd steered clear of him since that terrible morning, she had texted back with a simple Safe travels.

Upon entering the trailer, she flicked on the light. She walked into her office and booted up Cole's laptop. After sticking in her flash drive, Ruth opened the market report she'd created from the bid draft. She needed to print it out for the meeting she had lined up with a competitor.

Next week she'd find out if it might be worth selling her husband's business. The one she'd been so sure of keeping. Was this the right thing to do? She kept telling herself that gathering information was the wisest course to a solid decision, but it still felt wrong. All wrong. Was that sense from God or her own trepidation?

She hovered over the print button, her insides roiling.

The office door suddenly opened, and she nearly jumped out of her skin. What if it was Bo?

Feeling caught, she called out a shaky-sounding "Hello?"

Frank stuck his head into her office. "It's just me."

Relief flooded through her. "What's up?"

"I was going to ask you the same. Everything okay?"

"Yeah, sure. Why?" Ruth felt her face heat.

She'd never been good at telling fibs. She was far from okay. The last few days, she'd been a mess. She was still a mess.

Frank stepped farther into the office, looking concerned. "I was driving by and saw your car. I don't know, I got the feeling something was wrong. I might be prying where I shouldn't, but something is definitely wrong between you and Bo."

"What makes you think so?" Ruth evaded the question.

"Because he looks like someone kicked the life out of him."

Ruth clenched her hands into fists, forced a deep breath and stretched out her fingers. She had to tell him.

Frank probably didn't know about Bo not securing the pull rope properly. Telling him would bring back that horrible day and likely change the relationship her foreman had with Bo Harris forever. But it might also pave the way for understanding why she might sell.

Clearing her throat, which had become so very tight, Ruth forged ahead. "Bo didn't secure the rope on the tree that killed Cole."

Frank looked confused, then angry. "Who told you that?"

"Bo did."

Frank sat down in one of the chairs in front of her desk, his expression solemn. "Ruth, I checked the line myself. Because of the size of that tree and the trouble surrounding it, we used more than one rope. I made sure they were all secured. Bo didn't forget a thing. He had it right. That tree just turned wrong. I don't know if Cole miscalculated the cut or what, but it wasn't the fault of any improperly secured line."

Ruth digested the news, and it made her queasy. "Why would Bo think he caused Cole's death?"

"I don't know." Frank's eyes clouded over like a man haunted by the memory. "Bo performed CPR on Cole for at least fifteen minutes before first responders arrived."

"Bo did the CPR?" That was news to Ruth.

Frank had simply told her that they'd done CPR when he'd called her about Cole's accident. About his death. She'd assumed Frank had performed CPR but never asked him to be sure. She'd never wanted to cause her foreman pain by going back to that moment in time. The strange look on his face at the funeral, when she'd thanked him profusely for everything he'd done for Cole, made sense now.

"Bo did everything he could, but Cole was gone."

Stunned, Ruth sat perfectly still, staring as if trying to picture the accident and Bo's part in attempting to save her husband. Why hadn't he told her any of this?

Because she wouldn't listen. She wouldn't even return his calls. Her heart broke in two.

"I'm sorry, Ruth."

She looked up. "Thank you for telling me. What I don't understand is why Bo would think it was his fault. He never even mentioned that he was the one who had performed CPR."

Frank stood. "He was pretty shaken up. I'm sure it's something he doesn't want to talk about."

"Did Bo attend Cole's funeral?" Ruth was grasping at straws, trying to figure out why Bo would take on such culpability.

"He did. He sat in the back."

Was it any wonder that Bo didn't talk to her or offer his condolences? He blamed himself for everything that happened that day. He'd carried that guilt around all this time.

Ruth felt sick. She might have sold the business had Frank not stopped in to check on her. If he hadn't been driving by—

"Ruth, are you sure you're okay? You look a little pale."

She gave her foreman a wan smile. "I'll be fine, I just— Thank you for coming in and—" She blew out a breath. "Thank you for telling me all this."

He nodded. "I'll be on my way, then. Call me if you need anything."

"Okay. Thanks, Frank."

"See you next week."

"Yes, next week." Ruth watched her foreman leave as if she was frozen in place. Numb.

She glanced at the clock. It was nearly three. Bo might be at his mom's by now, but he might still be on the road. This wasn't something she could talk to him about over the phone. She didn't relish a two-and-a-half-hour drive in waning daylight on New Year's Eve either. Too many revelers might be on the roads.

Ruth hung her head and prayed for an opportunity to approach Bo. She didn't want to wait until after New Year's. She'd misjudged him, and for that, she was truly sorry. But what else could she have done, considering what he'd told her? He was as much to blame. She closed her eyes.

If only she'd heard him out, answered one of his calls. She owed Bo Harris an apology.

The computer screen had gone dark, so she clicked on the mouse, exited her document and powered it down. Pulling out the flash drive, she thought maybe tomorrow, if the weather held, she'd head toward Bo at his mom's.

Or maybe she should just call him and arrange to meet somewhere. This wasn't exactly a conversation to have where his mom might overhear. Regardless of where or when, Bo had some explaining to do, and this time, she'd listen. She needed to hear it all, and there were some things he needed to hear from her as well.

Chapter Fifteen

Bo gathered up his overnight duffel and exited the apartment. He didn't want to go to his mom's, but it would be better than staying here, sulking all weekend. And sulk, he would.

Losing Ruth hurt far worse than his breakup with Sheri. He didn't remember his heart aching quite this much. But then, regret seared his insides too. He kept replaying the day Cole died through his mind, but the answers remained the same. He was at fault.

Coming down the steps, he spotted Ruth's minivan, and his gut twisted into a ball of dread. For three days, they'd managed to come and go without running into each other. He'd known they'd have to resolve things to a point on Monday, but seeing her now threw him off-kilter.

It was too late to run back up the stairs like the coward he was; she'd spotted him before she turned into the driveway. Instead of parking near the garage, Ruth pulled diagonally in front of his truck, blocking his exit.

She got out and looked ready to do battle.

That she'd wait until he was ready to leave to discuss what he'd wanted to tell her three days ago grated on his nerves. He kept his voice even. "What are you doing?"

"I didn't think you'd still be here." She blew out a breath.

Was that relief he heard?

"I had a nail in my tire that needed fixed in town." What was with the chitchat?

"We need to talk."

No kidding. "Now?"

"Bo, I may have jumped to conclusions, but you weren't exactly honest with me. Can we go upstairs?"

He narrowed his gaze. What was she talking about? "I didn't lie to you, Ruth. I just didn't tell you the whole truth."

She rolled her eyes. "Isn't that the same thing? Only you were wrong."

"Wrong?"

"Can we please go upstairs and not talk in the driveway?" Her voice had risen a notch.

He felt safer in the driveway.

He glanced at the house. It didn't look like anyone was home, but Nora's car was parked in the garage. "What about your boys?"

With her hand on her hip, Ruth seemed to be

running out of patience. "Ethan is at a friend's house for the night. I'll let Nora know where I am and meet you upstairs, okay?"

"All right." Bo turned and headed back up the steps.

Entering the apartment, he wondered what she'd meant by *he was wrong*. Wrong about what? He dropped his duffel on the floor and headed for the woodstove. The apartment was chilly, and since it appeared he wasn't going anywhere anytime soon, he might as well keep busy while he waited.

After slipping out of his coat and tossing it over a chair, Bo crouched down by the hearth made of brick. Gathering up some kindling, he opened the stove door and tossed the sticks inside. Then he lit a long match and held it under the pile, glad when the flame caught on the corner of the dry wood.

Once the kindling was burning pretty well, he tossed in a couple of small logs, shut the door and stood. Rubbing the back of his neck, Bo considered calling his mom. He'd promised to text her when he left, but depending on what happened in the next few minutes, he might not leave at all.

Taking his cell phone out of his back pocket, he texted his mom that something had come up and it didn't look like he'd make it tonight. He promised to call later. With that done, he paced the apartment and waited. Was there a chance of making things right? What had he been wrong about?

Ruth gave a quick knock before walking in. She looked nervous.

And that made him nervous. "Want something to drink?"

"No." She stepped closer. Her hands clenched into fists, only to unclench and repeat. "Bo, you secured that rope."

Surprised at the conviction in her voice, he asked, "How do you know that?"

"Because Frank told me that he checked all the lines and they were secure."

"Frank?"

She looked impatient. "I went into the office, and he was driving by and checked on me. I asked him."

"I don't know what to say," Bo whispered. He'd been so sure. He'd been so afraid of the answer that he hadn't asked Frank.

"I wouldn't listen before, but I am now. I need to hear you tell me what happened that day."

Bo took a deep breath. "I didn't think I got the tension right. I vividly remember the pull rope going slack. Then the tree turned. I shouted out a warning, but the other line snapped, and that huge trunk fell where it wasn't supposed to, clipping another tree and causing a thick branch to fall and slam right into Cole."

Ruth closed her eyes as if seeing it, too, but then she looked at him and spoke in a soft voice. "Why would you think the fault was yours?"

A kernel of hope popped inside him.

He looked at her. "I envied him, you know. Cole had a family he loved and a good, honest business. He talked of you all the time. Do you even realize how happy you made him?"

Her eyes teared up. "We had a good marriage."

Exactly. Something he'd always wanted.

He squeezed his forehead, shielding his eyes, but the vision that was etched into his memory ran like a filmstrip across his mind. "Seeing that line go slack, I thought it was my error. My failure to keep Cole safe."

"It wasn't your job to keep Cole safe! He knew the risks, but he was careful. That's why he took Frank on the dangerous jobs. He trusted Frank with his life. Frank said it was an accident, that maybe Cole had miscalculated the cut. If that were so, could that have caused the line to go slack?"

He considered it. "Maybe…"

Ruth drew closer. "It wasn't your fault."

All these months he'd been uncertain, but his gut had pronounced him guilty. Maybe, because he had envied everything Cole had, he'd internalized the trauma he'd witnessed as guilt. As something he'd done wrong. If only he'd talked to Frank.

Ruth stepped even closer. "I almost sold the business. I have a meeting next week with a larger logging company."

That brought his head up with a snap. "What? Why?"

Tears ran down her cheeks now. "I didn't trust my feelings for you, and after you asked if I'd accept your deal if I'd known this—well, I didn't trust you either." Ruth dashed her tears away, but more fell.

Bo closed the short distance between them and wrapped his arms around her. "Oh, Ruth…"

She was crying in earnest now. "I'm so sorry."

He cradled her head against his chest. "I'm sorry too. Sorry for not double-checking with Frank. For not telling you at the beginning."

And then it dawned on him what she'd said. He drew back and lifted her chin so he could look into those golden brown eyes of hers. "What feelings?"

She gave him a soggy-sounding laugh. "I didn't mean to and I didn't want to—but I'm afraid I've fallen in love with you."

Hope filled him as he brushed back her red hair with his fingers. "I'm glad—because I love you, Ruth Miller. I think I fell in love with you at the diner, when you wouldn't share my fries."

"I couldn't because it wasn't a date—"

He covered her lips with his own, cutting off her laughter. Bo kissed her thoroughly but held himself in check. They might be legally married, but they were still far from wed. He hoped to remedy that soon.

Pulling back, he loved the way she opened her eyes to reveal a dreaminess he'd not soon forget. "I want to date you."

"Haven't we sort of been doing that?"

"No. Not really. That was business-centered. We can take our time, make sure you're ready and the boys are too." He cleared his throat. "Marry me, Ruth. Make our marriage deal real before God and our families. I'll wait for as long as it takes."

Ruth grinned and held out her hand. "It's a deal. I think we can go with a verbal contract this time."

"Real cute." Bo laughed, feeling lighter than he had in a long time. He took her hand and reached for her other one, giving both a squeeze. "I prayed for this, Ruth. I asked God to make a way for us, and He did."

She got all misty-eyed but smiled. "I should have gone to God first thing, but I jumped ahead, ready to tackle it all. I was so mad. I do that, you know. I bulldoze my way through things without taking time to really listen."

He lifted her hair, running his fingers through it. "Must be true, the red-hair thing."

She gave him a playful shove. "You have no idea. I need to get dinner started. Will you stay or go to your mom's?"

"I'm staying. In fact, I have to give my mother a call."

"I'll go, then. But come for dinner."

"Of course." Then he chuckled. "What are you making?"

"Meat loaf. You'll have to tell me how it stacks up against the diner."

"You've got some stiff competition there." He winked.

Ruth's eyes glowed. "Consider the challenge accepted."

Watching her leave, he hoped their wait to wed wouldn't be too long.

Later that evening, Ruth sat on the couch in the family room, leaning against Bo. His head was back, and Ruth knew by his even breathing that he'd fallen asleep.

Bruno lay stretched out against Bo's other side, and Owen was curled up under a knitted throw just beyond, fast asleep. Nora sat in the recliner, her eyes drifting closed. The fire had burned down to glowing embers in the woodstove.

Ruth yawned.

At this rate, none of them would make it to midnight to watch the ball drop in Times Square on TV.

Nora drifted into a snore, then jerked awake. "That's it. I'm headed for bed. Do you want me to take Owen upstairs with me?"

"No, I'll take him up." She had a feeling Owen might not want to sleep in his room without Ethan. Even with Bruno. She'd have both little ones in with her tonight. "Good night, Nora."

Her mother-in-law leaned down and kissed her forehead. "I'm glad things worked out."

"Me too."

Thankfully, she'd told Nora little, but the woman had known there was something wrong between her and Bo. It humbled her that Bo had been the one to pray for them. That God would make a way, and He had.

Bo shifted, waking up. "I don't think I'll make it to midnight."

"Yeah, everyone's bailing." Ruth sighed.

He sat up straight and rubbed his neck. "I'll take Bruno out."

She watched Bo carry the pup to the sliding door. Gently, he put Bruno out in the snow. It didn't take long. The dog returned to the door in no time.

Bo let him back in. "Good boy, Bruno."

The dog jumped up on the couch and settled down in the crook of Owen's bent knees.

"Would you like me to carry him upstairs?" Bo made the same offer as Nora.

Ruth shook her head. "I can manage. I'll walk you out."

"I'd like that."

Silently, they padded through the kitchen and into the laundry room. Ruth watched as Bo slipped into his boots and then his jacket, remembering her conversation with Frank. Bo might not like what she wanted to tell him.

"Bo…" Ruth hesitated, rallying the courage to continue.

"Yeah?" His gray eyes looked dark and sleepy. And so very dear.

"This might not be the best time to bring it up, but I can't let the year end without thanking you."

"For what?"

She reached for his hand. "Frank also told me that you were the one who performed CPR on Cole."

"Ruth—"

She placed her fingers against his lips. One day, maybe they'd really talk about it—but not now. "I just want you to know that I know you did everything you could."

His eyes filled. "It wasn't enough."

And that's when she knew for certain that Bo Harris hadn't wanted to buy into Miller Logging and Tree Service for his own interests or access to his trust fund. He'd done it for her, for her boys and Nora. Even for Frank. But most of all, Ruth believed Bo had saved the business to honor Cole.

"It was." She pulled Bo into her arms, feeling a sense of closure and peace. "I know it was."

They were going to heal. All of them, together.

Epilogue

◥

Two years later.

Ruth sat in the passenger seat of Bo's truck, gripping the ultrasound picture of their first child. A baby girl.

"Are we going to share the news?" Bo asked. "You know the boys will want to know."

Ruth didn't think twice. "Of course we are. Tonight at dinner. Consider it an early Christmas present."

Bo laughed. "Have you thought about names?"

Ruth knew the name the minute they'd found out they were having a girl. "I'd like to name her Kaarina, after your grandmother."

He reached for her hand and gave it a squeeze. "My mother will be so happy."

"And you?" Ruth asked.

"More than I thought possible." Bo pulled

onto their long, neatly plowed drive. "Home or office?"

"Home, please." Ruth smiled as they passed their newly built office, complete with a workshop and huge parking lot.

They'd landed the stewardship contract with the US Forest Service, and Frank was in the Hiawatha National Forest with a large crew. Bo would meet up with the smaller crew working on a residential selective cut.

The sight still filled her with awe, driving up to the farmhouse-style two-story Bo had built for them on his fifty acres. There were more bedrooms and an in-law suite for Nora. They also had a small barn with goats and chickens for Ethan, and even Owen helped collect the eggs. This past summer, Ruth had put in a garden.

Bo shifted into Park but kept the engine running. He leaned over for a kiss. "I'll see you later."

"Yes." She didn't tell him to be careful, as that went without saying. Every day was a gift they looked forward to opening together.

Ruth slipped out of the truck just as Nora was letting Bruno out the front door. She scooped up the dog and held him close until Bo drove off.

"How was your appointment?" Nora asked.

Ruth showed her the ultrasound. There was

no way she could wait till suppertime to tell. "The baby is healthy and a girl!"

Nora squealed with delight. "I've always wished for a girl to fuss over."

She recalled the Old Testament story of Ruth. In many ways, they were a modern-day testament to how God provides not only for needs but also heartfelt desires too.

"God heard your cry, *Naomi*." Ruth gave Nora a squeeze.

Her mother-in-law laughed. "He sure did. And our *Boaz* did good."

"He sure did."

Boothe Harris had done better than simply redeem Miller Logging and Tree Service. He'd brought them back from the brink of ruin and despair with love.

* * * * *

If you enjoyed this book by Jenna Mindel,
be sure to read her previous title,
A Soldier's Prayer,
which features Ruth's brother-in-law,
Cash Miller, as he helps Ethan and Owen
recover from the loss of their father.

Available now from Love Inspired!

Get 4 FREE REWARDS!

We'll send you 2 FREE Books plus 2 FREE Mystery Gifts.

FREE Value Over **$20**

Both the **Love Inspired**® and **Love Inspired**® **Suspense** series feature compelling novels filled with inspirational romance, faith, forgiveness, and hope.

Dear Reader,

First of all, thank you for picking up a copy of *A Secret Christmas Family*. It's the first in a new series that is centered on three widows and set in the Upper Peninsula of Michigan.

I hope you have enjoyed Ruth and Bo's modern-day marriage of convenience. I had a lot of fun tying in elements from one of my favorite Bible stories from the Old Testament book of Ruth. Reading Ruth again and again, I noticed how empowered both Naomi and Ruth were in spite of their losses. Neither waited around to be "redeemed" by Boaz. They pushed forward, making decisions that ultimately made a huge difference in their lives. And God blessed their choices.

My modern Ruth also pushes forward because she has to. Sometimes, life requires quick decisions. Fortunately, God promises all things work together for our good to those who love Him. We don't have to be afraid, even when we're hanging out there with no clear direction. As long as we place our trust in the Lord, we have nothing to fear.

I love to hear from readers. You can drop a note in the mail to PO Box 2075, Petoskey, MI

49770; or check out my website, www.jenna-mindel.com, which has a newsletter sign-up and link to my author Facebook page.

Maddie's story is up next… Stay tuned!
Jenna